D'oncle

What's that making my ears ring? And those bubbles exploding in the air, where do they come from? Am I a rind full of ineffable flesh or ineffable flesh girdled with rind? Where's my dog tail? Where are my maybug antennae? In heaven, hummingbirds cleaned my ears and eyes. Now I have to do it myself and little by little I've become quite skilled at it. In heaven, they wiped my bottom.

Eugène Savitzkaya

1

One night I woke up convinced that Uncle had escaped through the hole in the toilet, and when I opened the door I found that Uncle had indeed escaped through the hole in the toilet, and the floor tiles were scattered with toilet-paper confetti and hundreds of white feathers, as if someone had been having a pillow fight, and the toilet bowl and the walls were stippled with hairs and all sorts of excretions, and looking at the little porcelain hole I told myself, It can't have been easy for Uncle, and I wondered what I could do to get him out of there, after all Uncle must weigh a good two hundred pounds, and the first thing I did was take the toilet brush and shove it as far as I could down the hole, through the pool of stagnant brown water at the bottom, and I churned with the brush but it didn't do any good, Uncle might already have reached the septic tank, and as I churned the murky water sloshed onto the floor, carrying various repellent substances along with it, and I slipped and slid and my knees sank into the muck, and it felt almost like walking in the bay just after the tide has gone out, when it's all sludge and stench.

On all fours, drenched to my elbows in filth, I held my breath and bent over the toilet and stuck in my head, and I shouted Uncle's name into the water, and Uncle's name resounded in the depths but Uncle didn't answer, so I decided there was nothing more I could do to save him, and for once he'd have to find his way out on his own, and just then my brother opened the door behind me, and my brother was wearing a day-glo green T-shirt that just barely came down to his navel, and the T-shirt had *día libre* written on it, and my brother always sleeps in that T-shirt, and every thread of that T-shirt is impregnated with the scent of a flower, the scent of one of those delectable flowers that bloom in the yard in spring, and my brother is a fervent devotee of flowers and love, and he walked in with his eyes still half-closed from deep sleep, and I asked if he'd slept well, and my brother covered his nose with his T-shirt, and he reached out to help me up and said: Today it's your turn to clean, I did it yesterday.

2

Uncle sits with his stomach crammed between him and the table, and Uncle's stomach is so fat that it doesn't seem like a part of his body, it's like a package he's carrying, or a pet, but it should also be said that Uncle always sits up very straight despite what must be a very heavy stomach, his back obediently conforms to the chair back instead of the other way around, and his pet stomach always spills over the table a little, and it wiggles and gurgles just like an animal lying in his lap, and Uncle looks at the television's dark screen and says It's really too bad the TV isn't working.

The television's dark screen is dotted with fingerprints because back when the TV was working Uncle liked to press his fat index finger to it, and although the TV doesn't work anymore Uncle goes on looking at the dark screen until I bring him his dinner, as if he could still see some trace of his favorite shows in that void, and when I set down the plate Uncle rubs his hands and says No seagull today, and he chuckles, but I don't find it all that funny, so I smile, and I answer No, no seagull today, and Uncle says Pepper and I say In the kitchen, and Uncle gets up and heads off for the pepper, and his breathing is loud, and now and then he lets out a little cough.

Back at the table, he peppers his omelet by smacking the bottom of the plastic shaker with the palm of his hand till the pepper suddenly comes out, and once he considers his omelet sufficiently peppered, which is to say evenly coated with a layer of gray dust, Uncle sets about eating it, but with the first bite the pepper gets up Uncle's nose and tears come to his eyes, and he turns bright red, and that's when Uncle sneezes, very loudly the first time, and the second time even louder, not troubling to cover his mouth, and he spatters the table, and keeping calm I suggest that he blow his nose.

And if I can keep calm it's because I'm used to these explosions, but Uncle doesn't have time to take my advice, because another sneeze is coming, rising up from the depths, likely to devastate everything in its path, and I take it upon myself to hand him a Kleenex, and now Uncle's whole head has turned scarlet, as if it were about to burst, and so it does, yet again, and Uncle spews out a sizable wad of runny omelet, whereupon I allow myself to offer him a second piece of advice, not so calmly this time, which is that he would do well to go easy on the pepper if he can't handle it.

But Uncle is certain his sneezing fits have nothing to do with the pepper, he rejects my advice with a snort, as if it were founded in some weird crackpot theory, and all I can do is hand him another Kleenex, and he loudly blows his nose then gets up to toss the used Kleenex into the cold fireplace, and he comes back out of breath, visibly unsteady on his feet, and he sits down again, and he finishes his omelet, and he says it's a very good omelet, and along with the omelet there are slices of tomato and a piece of garlic-rubbed bread, and as always Uncle saves his favorite part for last, and he starts in on the bread, groaning, moaning, letting out little grunts of pleasure.

Uncle always sits in the spot nearest the television, and I always sit in the spot farthest from Uncle, and my brother, before he left us, took to sitting well away from the table, and away from Uncle and away from me, because he was happier eating on the couch, behind Uncle's back, and sometimes, in those not-so-long-ago days when the TV was working, Uncle watched the news as he ate, and when he watched the news he turned up the sound as loud as it would go, and the frightening, sensationalistic news dispensed by the tiny old television distracted him from his eating, and one of his favorite things was to comment on and exaggerate the stories being reported, and he said it was going to be 600 degrees out the next day, and he said a comet would soon graze the coast of Brittany, and he said the virus was spread by fly bites, and he said there were giant ticks on the Belgian border, and I knew my brother was finding it harder and harder to hear Uncle spout those absurdities, and sometimes my brother tried to explain to Uncle why he shouldn't believe everything they said on TV, but that's not how Uncle saw it, he said the world was more interesting this way, swollen, inflated, glutted with faraway, murderous happenings, like a low-budget disaster movie played over and over.

Eventually my brother gave up arguing with him and stopped watching the news, and at dinnertime, as Uncle sat hypnotized by the TV with his food going cold in front of him, I looked at my brother lost in the study of Uncle's head, which was topped by a big giant wart, and my brother narrowed his eyes to examine that unlovely sprout on Uncle's head, because strangely my brother has always taken a keen interest in that cranial wart, he can't take his eyes off it, and when he squints to inspect it more closely he looks like he's contemplating a menhir in the mist, and he can't help wrinkling up his face and showing his big teeth, and it doesn't do me any good to tell him again and again that he looks like a dope, good old habits are hard to shake, to quote Uncle, who doesn't much like me nagging my brother, to quote Uncle, who loves his nephew more than anything in this world.

It might be worth adding that we never sit facing Uncle, the spot across from Uncle being reserved for guests to be put to the test, my brother's new girlfriends for instance, and all sorts of young people who are too polite to protest, because eating across from Uncle means consenting to share his food, I mean consenting to the torrents of spit he shares with your face, Uncle's the talkative type, especially with first-time visitors, who need to be put at their ease.

When we were little we usually spent part of the summer at our grandparents' house, which when they died became Uncle's house, since Uncle is their son, but Uncle's house is also my mother's vacation house, since my mother is his sister, and she spends five weeks there every summer and two every winter, and to tell the truth the more time goes by the less we know whose house it is, and recently my Uncle, my brother, and I became what I would call involuntary housemates, or a commune of idlers, or a congregation of do-nothings, and we're not complaining.

Uncle's house is in a little hamlet looking onto the ocean, and it's a white house with pale blue shutters lashed by the salty wind from the bay, a house whose walls are being eaten away by the ivy we used to pull down every summer as a family activity, knowing there was no point, knowing the ivy would be back the next year, covering the walls with shadows and indelible stars, and of course we should have dealt with it earlier, should have kept an eye on that destructive greenery's growth, but in those days we were only vacationers, transients, part-timers, and we couldn't expect Uncle to see to that job, because Uncle likes ivy, he thinks it makes the house look like a haunted house, a deserted house in some remote backwater, and so the house goes on eroding in the remote backwater that is the hamlet, between two pastures grazed by horses with blue and red irises.

Even with the ocean so close, Uncle never goes swimming, he tells us the locals never swim, swimming's only for tourists, and anyway the water's full of liquid manure these days, full of pig dung and blue-green algae, none of which seems to bother the people who still swim in it, the tourists in question, who still fish in the mudflats where there used to be beautiful red crabs and spider crabs and where there are now only anonymous little crustaceans, translucent, as if worn down by the oily backwash, weary from picking their way through the wads of peat.

When we were that age when you only know your own age, we didn't know Uncle was already older, because all three of us, Uncle, my brother, and I, loved to play dress-up, and Uncle made us Indian headdresses and pirate swords, and he was always the one who handed out the toys or ran to the upstairs window to throw the boomerang to my brother who stood waiting in the yard, squinting, hands in the air, and often our uncle took us out walking by the bay, where he showed us how to gather whelks and how to swallow them raw, and he swallowed whelks with their shells, and winkles too, and razor clams, and seaweed, and octopuses, and Uncle was an ogre, and back then he was skinny and limp, but still strong enough to carry us on his back and still limber enough to hide under the hedge, and when we came out for vacation he spent whole days playing with us, he didn't have anything better to do, because he didn't yet have a job at the abbey, and he only stopped playing to take a drag on his cigarette, and the cigarette might have been the one thing that distinguished us from each other, him the uncle and us the children, the real children.

It must be twenty years since Uncle last went out to the bay, because to get to the bay you have to take a narrow path along the side of a hill, then go down a steep set of rocky steps, then trudge through the thickest silt in the world, and not for nothing do we call that path the path of adventure: the steps are covered with seaweed and lichen, and it can be very dangerous, very slippery, depending on how high the tide has come up the steps, but Uncle isn't the type to go clambering around on rocks anymore: he can hardly get down the stairs that lead to the living room.

You might say Uncle rappels down those stairs, since he sort of comes down them backward, leaning with all his weight on the banister, his face turned toward the steps and his bottom protruding toward the living room, not as a joke but because he has to lay his upper body on the banister while he finds his footing on his good leg, because of a steel plate that won't let him bend the other one, and the old ash wood creaks with his every move, and his every move raises a bunch of dust, and a little before the last step Uncle starts to stand upright again, which signals the imminent end of the laborious descent, and finally Uncle sets foot on the living room's tile floor, and then he can display himself in his favorite position: feet joined at the heels, toes pointing out, in a sort of contrapposto vaguely reminiscent of a ballerina at rest, which is when you realize that his stiffness and his limp come from a deformed hip, to which a big metal plate was screwed one day, and ever since that day Uncle limps and puffs and struggles to move, and also ever since that day, not being easily discouraged, Uncle slides over the living room's tile floor, he doesn't limp, he skates in his socks, with a certain grace actually, the grace of a ballerina or a rag mop.

Today Uncle's outdoor activities are limited to little walks around the yard, where sometimes, when the weather's good, he sets up a target and shoots arrows at it, or else he cuts the grass, or else he walks around on that grass to set out his mole traps.

Those mole traps are tube-shaped things that emit sound waves every forty seconds, waves that make moles run away and that human beings aren't supposed to be able to hear, so my brother and I may well have turned into moles, because our long roommatehood was punctuated every forty seconds by very audible stridulations whose source didn't stay mysterious for long, and since the traps also go off at night we begged Uncle to get rid of them, but Uncle can be stubborn, and he refused to hear our pleas, so maybe we got used to that horrible bleeping, unless we ended up turning into human beings.

When we were first roommates my brother had just fallen in love with a woman from Barcelona, and at night, in the dark, he strove and struggled to write love letters in Spanish, and he filled the vacant hours of his day listening to stories for beginning learners, once it was the story of a fat man who wanted to run a marathon and another time it was the story of a princess who didn't know how to ride a horse, and there's nothing my brother wouldn't do to learn Spanish, and he had plenty of time to learn, because we spent four months in Uncle's house, in Uncle's company, for reasons I don't entirely understand, and sometimes I got up at night to go pull out the mole traps, hoping Uncle wouldn't notice, but there's no getting around Uncle when it comes to his pursuit of his enemies the moles, and he would reset the traps at sunrise, beneath the curious eyes of the morning's first seagulls.

Uncle is a patient foe, who's waged more than one war of attrition and never given in to anger, he often says: Everyone has their enemies, and his enemies are the moles and our enemies, as if by chance, bear the names of skin diseases, cankers or scabies for example, and my brother long did battle with parasites, with the ants and aphids that besieged our four stunted fruit trees, our four fruit trees that caused us such worry, because the fact is that a tree in a yard faces a great many dangers, an observation that Uncle judged far too alarmist, and with his pendulum in his hand Uncle assured us the trees would survive the wind and the rust, and he made that diagnosis as master of the pendulum. He would never dream of proclaiming himself master of the pendulum, he only said, more modestly, that he practiced radiesthesia, but we, his heirs, found that humility excessive, and we often called him master of the pendulum, because you should know that one time, thanks to his pendulum, Uncle found the chess set that was lost in the clutter of the attic, and another time, again thanks to his pendulum, Uncle found his uncle, dead, but his usually infallible pendulum was wrong on this score, I mean about the trees, one glance was enough to see they weren't at all well: Uncle went on saying everything would be fine, and he also asked us to stop looking so gloomy, as if there had been some loss of life or limb.

3

My brother was born in August, and when August comes Uncle never forgets to buy him a birthday present, and often, by Uncle's own admission, the present was pondered long and hard in the aisles of the supermarket, because Uncle wants to make his nephew happy, and he's convinced his own preferences will never steer him wrong, and Uncle starts from the principle that his nephew shares his tastes in all things, as if both of them, uncle and nephew, were cast from the same mold, which is why he always buys the birthday present in pairs: two *Rambo* DVDs, two butter knives with a handle in the form of a Breton ermine, two skull T-shirts in extra large, and when my brother politely informs Uncle that the T-shirt is a thousand times too big for him Uncle answers that it doesn't matter, because this way he can keep growing inside it, because this way he can keep growing inside it forever, and maybe Uncle thought he and his nephew had the same build, unless to Uncle getting older means growing ever bigger.

Uncle and my brother don't exactly have the same build, and they aren't the same age, and they don't have the same hair: Uncle has almost none left, just two sparse little tufts on either side of his head, whereas my brother is very hairy, a beautiful brown mane, thick eyebrows, and my brother has a driver's license and Uncle doesn't, and when Uncle was a teenager he owned a scooter that he often put in the ditch on his way home from the nightclub, and when those days were over Uncle opted for a moped that with comical masculine pride he calls "my hog," as if it were a Harley, whereas the hog in question can't go over twenty, maybe twenty-five miles an hour, and even then only on a downhill, but Uncle says it's perfect this way, because the police are everywhere these days, and for all his trepidation about the police Uncle seems to take immense pleasure in straddling his hog, and he looks enormous as he putts away on his tiny bike.

Sometimes, in the old days, he even left his helmet's visor open so he could smoke a cigarette, and sometimes, since the visor was open and it was summer and Uncle was riding his hog, a wasp would fly into his helmet, and more than once he was stung on the cheek or neck, but very fortunately Uncle isn't allergic to wasp stings, and Uncle explains that all you have to do to treat the sting is stop by the side of the road, find a tree away from prying gazes, urinate into the palm of your hand, then vigorously massage the site of the sting, an old army technique, he says.

The day Uncle learned he'd been accepted into the army was a great day, and his father was very proud to learn that his son would be a grenadier, very proud and maybe even a little surprised, and the morning he was going to set off Uncle and his father celebrated the big event in a bar near the Gare de l'Est, and they drank to the health of the grenadiers, the paratroopers, the legionnaires, the big boys.

Uncle talks about the army with no particular emotion, it's just something he did in his life, like his horticulture course at the Château d'Arnouville, like his internships on the sets of the ORTF, and like that astonishing stint as an archivist for an insurance company near the Marcadet-Poissonniers metro stop.

I've always found it hard to picture Uncle as an archivist, but I also have some trouble imagining him as a soldier, because Uncle isn't the warrior type, far from it, and that's what surprises you when you hear him talk in a vaguely martial tone about AK47s, lead shot, Luger cartridges, and that's what surprises you when you hear him recount in a vaguely boastful tone his tales of barracks life and three-day leaves, the way I suppose others recall their battlefield exploits and their benders, and Uncle too replays the same memories over and over.

Uncle says he could never keep in step with the others, he was always a little behind, one two, one two, like an overweight crab, left right, left right, that's how you were supposed to walk, one step after the other like everyone else, and Uncle is always telling us how, during a parade, the corporal halted the regiment, and how the corporal wanted them to get rid of that faggot who's singing in that high-pitched voice, and how the corporal yelled Where's the faggot?, and Uncle tells how he eventually understood and stepped forward amid gales of laughter, and how he too was laughing amid the gales of laughter that were pouring down on him, and when I hear that story I always imagine how the corporal must have stood in front of Uncle and how he must have yelled at him, and how the corporal used Uncle as an example to make it clear to the conscripts that not even the tiniest nub of eccentricity would be tolerated, that they had to keep in step both literally and figuratively, it was better for everyone, and that was a lesson they could use all their lives, and Uncle never fails to specify that it was him singing in that high-pitched voice, just in case my brother and

I didn't understand, and he always laughs when he tells that story, and we laugh along as if we were there with him in the ranks, all three of us soldiers in the service of our fatherland.

Every summer my mother spends her three-week vacation dreaming of all the wonderful things she'll be able to do someday, maybe soon, who knows, when she moves into her parents' house, when she retires, after the labor, maybe soon, who knows, the restful reward.

And my mother will buy herself a couple of goats she'll keep penned in a corner of the yard, and they'll give her milk that as if by magic will become cheese, and she'll have beehives as well, and she'll plant carnations on the south side, and Pierre de Ronsard roses, and camellias, and magnolias, and she can even take up painting again, and she can also get a dog, or two dogs, or three cats, in addition to the cats she already has, which have thyroid problems, and then best of all she'll have time, time to sleep, and time to read the books that apparently you have to have read once you've reached a certain age, and time to walk on the path, to look at the sea, that glorious panorama, and my mother also says she's going to add on to the house someday, which reminds her of the blueprints that must be lying around somewhere in the clutter of the attic, the blueprints without which she can't undertake any building projects because without those blueprints, which as it happens she's never really looked for, she won't know where the plumbing lines are buried, she might put a hole in a big pipe while she was digging the new foundation with her little hands, and besides, on top of that, she knows next to nothing about the laws governing additions to coastal houses, is that even allowed? where do you go to find out? and to think that she'll also have to deal with the car, and its registration, and the certificate of compliance, and the official inspection, and the tax forms, and her brother who she's going to have to live with someday, and her brother who someday won't be able to walk anymore, and her brother whose diapers she's going to have to change someday, and my mother feels like she's going to throw up.

But my mother reassures herself: she doesn't even have the money for her cats' radioiodine therapy, and she's still got, at the very least, ten years of work to endure.

Uncle and my mother both spent their childhood in Montmagny, outside of Paris, and their memory of it is at once happy and distant, and a few years ago we went to Montmagny with my mother and we saw an uninteresting gray city, and we stood in front of a low-income housing project, and my mother pointed at windows, she wasn't sure, she couldn't quite remember which room was Uncle's and which was hers, or if it was the apartment above or the apartment below, and then finally she said Oh I don't know anymore and she seemed disappointed in herself, and we turned around, we walked down the street to the station, and just across from the station there was a sign, and the sign said that the city of Montmagny was the sister city of another city of Montmagny, in Quebec, and my mother said she didn't know that, and that sign didn't used to be there, and one summer evening at dinner my mother asked her brother if he knew Montmagny was sister cities with another Montmagny, in Quebec, but Uncle hadn't heard about it either, and to him there was only one Montmagny, the one where he learned to play the drums, and the one where thanks to his friend Manu he discovered what he still today calls "good music," which is to say the heavy metal of the 1980s.

Manu was Uncle's childhood friend, and he was also his neighbor, he lived in the apartment upstairs with his parents, and with his four sisters, and with his two brothers, and Manu and Uncle, both of them little last-borns, inevitably found each other one gray Wednesday afternoon in the stairway, after which I picture them as inseparable, and Manu is the only friend Uncle's ever told us about, and Manu not only introduced Uncle to good music, he also taught him a certain demeanor characteristic of devotees of that sort of good music, and in the photos from those days you can see Uncle wearing a pin-laden jean jacket, cowboy boots, a bandana, and over the years since the Manu era Uncle has developed a very particular notion of heavy metal, his own notion, unorthodox if you like, a notion that doesn't have much to do with that slightly outmoded musical genre, I think, because Uncle classifies more or less everything he likes as heavy metal, and so associates it with those glorious years he spent learning from and laughing with his friend Manu.

To Uncle, heavy metal is the Beauregard housing project in Montmagny, at the corner of the Rue des Acacias and the Rue d'Épinay, and heavy metal is afternoons with Manu in his room, and heavy metal is the first VCRs, and records shoplifted from the Fnac store in the Rosny 2 mall, and twenty-four hours in jail, and heavy metal is folding cots and used chewing gum hidden in slippers, it's looking at Manu's sisters in the shower, it's farting really loudly, it's the burning yoghurt cup prank, it's cutting the brake lines on the bicycle, it's smoking, it's drinking, a lot, until you fall over, until you throw up, while listening to Iron Maiden, all just for laughs.

Uncle doesn't play the drums anymore, his cymbals are rusting in one corner of his room, under a water-stained Iron Maiden poster, but recently Uncle developed a passion for archery, and two or three times a year, when we visit him during vacations, he asks us to take him to the sporting-goods store, where he buys targets and bows, and a few arrows, and medals that he never fails to solemnly award himself at the end of a successful session.

And when I ask Uncle whatever became of Manu Uncle turns evasive, and he starts talking about heavy metal, and he drones on and on about the old days, but all the same I managed to worm a little information out of him one day, and I know Manu tried several times to get hold of Uncle after he moved to Brittany, and I know Uncle didn't want to get back to him, so it would seem they didn't part on very good terms, and Uncle secretly told me he didn't want Manu breezing in here, which seems unlikely, given that at last word Manu is stuck in a wheelchair.

It was in 1992 that Uncle and his parents left the suburbs of Paris to move to the country, Uncle was twenty-five at the time, and my mother had already been living in Switzerland for ten years, and I'd just been born, and it was in July 1992 that Uncle, my grandmother, and my grandfather set down their bags in Brittany, as they did every summer, with their sun hats and wool sweaters, only this time they didn't go back, and my grandfather set up a bedroom for his son, on the second floor, adjoining his workshop, and soon my grandmother was bemoaning the cozy relationship that blossomed between those two.

Once the family was settled in Brittany my grandfather thought he should see about a job for his son, who was getting close to thirty. It took almost five years of intense searching to find him a job as a gardener at the abbey. Five years of father and son trawling the neighboring villages, stopping in every café and PMU to inquire into employment opportunities for a young gardener, and getting to know the locals, because they were banking on word-of-mouth. From morning on, my grandfather and Uncle made it a rule to overlook no OPEN sign and no step in the protocol: they walked in, stood at the bar and drank as many toasts as politesse required, telling everyone that their work was looking for work, until one fine day, five years after the start of the quest, their efforts paid off and they raised a glass to the long walkways and magnificent vegetable gardens of the abbey.

Uncle had to upgrade his appearance when he went to work for the nuns, because he and his father had spent a long time digging up that job, and he was supposed to keep it for as long as he could: gone, from one day to the next, were the inverted crosses and studded wristbands, the long hair and Vercingetorix mustache, and it was then that Uncle came up with his own personal uniform, a pair of sweatpants and a T-shirt, which Uncle has stuck to ever since, no matter the weather, as if he knew only one single season and it was a warm one.

To look at his aged sweatpants, worn down by years of a not particularly athletic lifestyle, stained with all sorts of fluids, you might think comfort is Uncle's only concern, but that isn't exactly true, because Uncle does devote some attention to his choice of garb, as is expressed above all by his T-shirts, some of which proclaim his preferences in music and literature (the punk band Les Ramoneurs de Menhirs, Hulk), while others, bought at the village market, bear obscure messages, a robot raising a middle finger for instance, and for a reason that slightly escapes me Uncle also likes the T-shirts he gets from Erwan, one of his co-workers, and often the T-shirts Erwan gives him are too small and pretty ugly, and they all have logos on them—EDF, Jardiland, Mr. Bricolage, Moto Évasion Plancoët—and those T-shirts are, if I understand correctly, rejects from a collection organized by Erwan in aid of needy Nepalese, and Uncle wears those T-shirts with pride, like a sign of fidelity to Erwan and his Nepalese who live somewhere in a country called Nepal, says Uncle, a Nepal so far away that Erwan has to fly when he goes there every year, a land Uncle knows only secondhand, from the stories Erwan tells him as they harvest potatoes and rake up dead leaves.

Uncle hates hoodies. I don't know why he hates hoodies, and I also don't know why he bought himself a hoodie anyway, because, I forgot to say, Uncle does own a jacket for cold days and long scooter outings, and as it happens that jacket happens to be a jacket with a hood, and that problem did not long withstand Uncle's cunning, and his solution was definitive, efficient, and cost-free: he simply tucks that ugly hood under the thick fabric of the collar, and he let me in on that little secret himself when I asked him about the strange lump on his back, created by that cursed hood, and then I offered to cut it off for him, because it made him look like a Medieval hunchback in a Hieronymus Bosch painting, but he said no, it's just perfect this way.

4

I can't call up a clear image of my grandmother, but I did know her, for a few summers, and from those few summers I still remember a haggard woman with sunken cheeks, flecks of foam always at the corners of her mouth, and I especially remember that she scared us a little, my brother and me, with her way of wanting us to taste her strawberries and cookies, there was something aggressive about it, something insistent, something that put us off, and I remember she wore clothes made from fabric remnants she'd picked up here and there, and crocheted scarves, and funny plastic earrings, and I remember my grandfather liked to call her Belette, and I know her makeup cases full of crushed lipstick tubes are still stored in the attic, and that's more or less all that's left of her, and—according to a family legend to be taken with a grain of salt—she was once Brigitte Bardot's stand-in, and twenty years ago Uncle and my mother sailed out from the Crozon peninsula, where my grandmother came from, and scattered her ashes, and Uncle remembers that he and my mother also took advantage of that excursion to eat a nice pot of mussels.

Back in the Montmagny days my grandfather built sets for the ORTF, so he was sort of a handyman, and in his workshop there are still remnants of a lifetime of little tinkerer jobs: old set parts turned into furniture, lamps with extravagant shades, phonographs, unplayable musical instruments, all kinds of dusty old stuff, and with all that stuff and its characteristic mushroom-bed smell his workshop seems just like the back room of a provincial antique store.

In 1992 my grandfather gave it all up to devote himself to paintings of naked women on the beach, which apparently kept him going for ten years or so, because the seven hundred canvases of naked women on the beach stored in the workshop are, among other things, what remains of my grandfather, and apart from that I have a memory, a vague memory, of a warm, whimsical man, and I know he died of cirrhosis when I was eight, and in the photos you see him dressed in white, with a scarf around his neck, a chinbeard, long hair, a pipe in his mouth, every inch the painter of naked women on the beach.

My grandmother, who didn't have a car and refused to ride a bicycle, was completely dependent on my grandfather, and she sent him to do the shopping in the village, and my grandfather, the painter of naked women on the beach, the gentle dreamer, the smoker of pipes and wearer of white kaftans, had to make several trips to bring back everything the household required, now it was dish liquid they'd run out of, now the noontime roast beef, now a prescription, and then my grandfather would complain, all this coming and going quickly got old, but in the end he always submitted to his wife's demands, as long as she let the little one come with him, the little one being Uncle.

The Vieille Auberge still exists today, but we never go there because it's an especially sordid PMU, probably more or less what it was twenty or thirty years ago when my grandfather and Uncle used to stop off there on the way home from the roast-beef run, and Uncle talks with deep emotion about those little jaunts, which he counts among his most precious memories, and he acts them out for us, with both voice and gesture, sparing us not one of the memorable feats of the Vieille Auberge "clan."

There was Chouquette, there was Jacky, there was Caniche, there was the Baron, there was the Druid, who was Uncle's uncle, and Caniche always started off with a pastis, and Chouquette and Jacky had already been there a while and were on their fourth glass of red wine, and a Suze for the Baron, and a Picon-and-beer for the Druid, And a beer for papa and a beer for me, Uncle recounts, segueing into a high-pitched, distant voice to imitate the Baron who'd had half his face removed because of mouth cancer, no lips, no teeth, two holes where his nose used to be, but no lack of good humor, Uncle tells us, chuckling at the mere memory of that jolly old soul.

But with nothing in your stomach, and so early in the morning, the drinks hit you fast, and

Uncle loves to explain the fool-proof technique he devised to keep up with the clan's vigorous pace: all it took was two fingers down his throat in the secrecy of the bathroom, and I wonder if it was at the Vieille Auberge that Uncle developed his habit of keeping things quiet, and once he'd taken care of himself, to the indifference of all, Uncle went back to the bar where the Druid was now singing Wehrmacht anthems, and some of the clan joined in while others feigned indignation, but Uncle assured us it was all in good fun, and they had fun like that for some time, all of them together, and Uncle and my grandfather were always late coming home.

When they did, Uncle and my grandfather got a good scolding, my grandmother said the pair of them were as good as a bunch of lushes, every one worse than the last, and I don't know if my grandmother included herself in that chain of lushes all trying to outdo each other, but Uncle implies that his mother was no slacker, because in the back of the big armoire there was a bottle of nice strong cordial prescribed by the village bonesetter in case of anxiety, and their lateness made her very anxious, and my grandfather and grandmother ended up agreeing that there was a line at the butcher's and in any case roast beef is meant to be eaten cold.

Uncle likes to tell us about Jessy, the nomad, the rebel who slept on Chouquette's couch, and the Baron, the impeccably dressed man with no face, who drove to the Vieille Auberge every morning and didn't leave until evening, just be fore the owners, and he lists the causes of their deaths like one last barroom story, cirrhosis, anal cancer, kidney failure, and suicide too—Jessy, the nomad, the rebel—and when Uncle tells us those stories from the Vieille Auberge he always seems overcome by nostalgia, nostalgia for a time when, to hear him tell it, there was no such thing as a roadside sobriety check.

Unfortunately, I never met most of the clan, only Caniche, who rented an apartment to my mother one summer when there was nowhere else to rent near her parents' house, and in my memory Caniche was a very quiet man, tall and thin like the Druid, and strangely, and contrarily to the adage, his dog was his absolute opposite, it was huge, with thick, glossy fur, and it didn't smoke, and it was in perfect health, and his dog was named Brume, but that was just a short-term thing, and my grandmother left this earth right after my grandfather's last breath, I don't remember exactly when, but they weren't very old, just past sixty.

5

Ever since their father died my mother and Uncle have remembered him with a sort of reverence, and they made a kind of funerary scarecrow that's supposed to be him, and what it is is a bolster pillow dressed in a kaftan and a sailor's cap that presides over the attic, and actually I suspect it was my uncle who initiated the project of the paternal effigy, because the handyman spirit was passed down from father to son, along with a fondness for practical jokes, and I'm not sure Uncle is capable of changing a lightbulb but I know he likes doing little repairs and renovations, for example he regularly restuffs the armchairs with newspaper, or when the sole of his old tennis shoe starts to come away he sticks it back on with super glue.

My mother thinks my brother and I communicate in a strange language, a sort of pidgin that's ours alone, in which she thinks she hears a Helvetian singsong of the kind that's always annoyed her in German Swiss children, who she finds so different from French kids, less polite, fussier about food, and like them, she claims, we swallow our words, we chew them with our mouths open, we maim them, some of the syllables stay stuck to our uvulas, and to make it worse we talk so fast that she can't understand us, and she says we've always talked to each other that way, and she also wishes she could have made up an incomprehensible language with her brother, a secret language, but there was no way, because even though she and her brother have always spoken the same language they've never spoken the same language, for example when my mother asks Uncle to weed the front yard he takes out the garbage, and when she asks him to pass the mustard he races off to the supermarket, and my mother understands that Uncle understands only what he wants to understand, not to mention that he never calls her, her life doesn't interest him, it's probably the age difference, my mother tells herself, that's got to be it, the age difference, that must be why she's never really managed to understand her brother.

My brother and I have the same flaws, and the first of those flaws is that we have eczema, which is to say that, rather than protecting us from external aggressions, our skin itches endlessly, and it goes rough and dry like old crocodile leather, and it cracks and it fissures and it furrows, because over the years raking that defective skin has become as natural and unconscious as breathing, and some people say our skin is too fine for this world, that we're allergic to it, to this world, and those people might be right, I don't know, but what I do know is that we have another flaw, my brother and me, and that second problem is that we share the same profession, and that profession is translating instructions for animal food: ostrich ears for dogs, horse tendons for cats, beef chews for rabbits, goose sinew for axolotls.

Over thirty years of single living Uncle has had time to develop certain habits that today form the very core of his existence, the core or maybe the structure, the solid armature that holds up the essential, the unexpected, and the rest, and among those habits are some that have a particular, vital importance, which are very naturally those connected to what my uncle calls his bachelor grub, his diet in other words, which is largely made up of andouille sandwiches wolfed down in the privacy of his room.

Uncle also claims to be the custodian of the time-honored recipe for calamari à l'armoricaine, a recipe that consists of frozen squid rings vaguely cooked in half a gallon of cheap red wine seasoned only with a pinch of pepper, a dish, I should add, reserved for special occasions, for honored guests, for first-time visitors, because Uncle likes to give all newcomers a lavish welcome, at least those who are too polite to refuse what they're so beamingly being offered, and when we suggest to Uncle that he add some garlic, and go a little lighter on the red wine, and have a look at the sell-by date on the squid, and also take a shower, just a little more often, a real shower, not just a swipe with a wet washcloth, no, a real cleaning from top to bottom, Uncle says simply no, he doesn't want to, he's sticking to his father's recipe.

In normal times, when Uncle was working, he washed once a week, and with any change in the routine, vacations for instance, Uncle stopped washing altogether, so when he didn't have work Uncle let his beard and hair grow, and he never changed clothes, which is to say that he slept in the clothes he'd worn to go to the supermarket or shoot his bow, and he woke up at seven at night and three in the morning, and he stuffed himself with cookies and slices of andouille, and he smelled bad, as you might expect, and he smoked, and he drank beer, but he never drank hard liquor, as he often stressed, and he did all that while watching a good horror movie, or reading a good crime novel, but apart from a few minor details it was the same in normal times, when, every Sunday afternoon at five, he ran a bath, and every Sunday afternoon at five Uncle slipped his fat, pale body, at once flabby and stiff, into the tiny bathtub, and I imagine that must have been a particularly tricky operation, which was a good reason to leave it for Sundays.

When I hear the opening splashes I can't help but picture Uncle as a big plastic doll, naked before the water-stained little mirror he shaves with, and when he emerges from the bathroom freshly shaved and perfumed, his cheeks and chin and sometimes even the top of his head are dotted with little cuts, and behind him he leaves a thick cloud of knockoff cologne, and after Uncle has been in the bathroom we often find a wad of brown-stained cotton on the floor or the rim of the sink, and no one knows where that mysterious compress comes from, or for how long or what part of Uncle's body compressed it, and without evidence or confession we can't say for sure, but we have our theory, and my brother and I thumb-wrestle to decide which of us will pick up the dreaded cataplasm, the revolting ectoplasm, and one day I'm the loser and another it's my brother, and it must be said that there are no winners in that game, but as of a few weeks ago, our minds are made up, we're not going to eat any more squid.

From our earliest childhood our mother made garlic compresses to put on our eyelids and under our arms but my brother and I went right on scratching ourselves, and sometimes we look at each other in horror, surprised and saddened by the wounds and scars we inflict on ourselves, surprised and horrified and saddened by our scabby, red, or livid skin, the result of years of compulsive scratching, and in the end, and after much hypothesizing, it seems there's no hope of discovering the cause of what we have no choice but to call our illness, and, we're both convinced, that hopelessness is no reason not to ponder and speculate and periodically pin the blame on pollen or mites, dust, damp, the fur of certain animals and the saliva of certain people, and when we run out of hypotheses, when our imagination starts to falter, we always come back to impatience, and you may ask What makes you impatient?, and I believe that's where we get close to our ailment's real cause, because nothing makes us impatient, that impatience is the impatience of nothingness, and that, we sense, is where it comes from, from nothingness, from the emptiness deep down inside us, from the stirring and throbbing of the emptiness inside us, and that's what turns us into these louse-infested beasts, these fleabags, these bundles of nerves that no balm can soothe, but enough whining, because it's also true that scratching when you have an itch, even if it's all the time, where you have an itch, even if it's everywhere, brings an intense pleasure and a deep satisfaction, and we could easily devote our days and weeks to it, reducing ourselves to sawdust and shavings with fingernails and rasps and anything else we might find at hand, never thinking of the consequences, not thinking of anything, thinking of nothing, the very nothing that binds my brother and me, the reason we're never at peace.

Uncle is by nature a peaceable man, and sometimes he sticks his head out the window like a hermit crab erupting from its shell, and you might think he's wanting to gaze on the glorious panorama that some envy him for, and you would be wrong, because nothing interests

Uncle less than the beauties of the landscape, sunsets, tempestuous seas, and the millions of stars leave him completely indifferent, what Uncle likes is action, which he doesn't see much of, often nothing more than a hedgehog crossing the yard, but as we were saying Uncle is by nature a peaceable man, and so satisfactory does he find the doings of the local fauna that at the slightest rustle he grabs his binoculars, a high-quality pair purloined from his army gear, and positions himself at his watchpoint, and then a rabbit goes by.

Not long ago Uncle's room was still off-limits to us, not because Uncle one day forbade us to enter his room—that's not really his style, no, it was more a sort of unspoken rule, a tacit accord as they say—and not long ago, when Uncle still got up in the morning for work, he locked the door to his room with a key and hid the key in one of my grandmother's jewelry cases, and we all knew where his hiding place was but none of us cared, no one would ever have thought of entering Uncle's lair in his absence, because that's how it is with real taboos, the kind the tribe's survival depends on, the idea of transgressing that law never entered our minds.

Uncle's uncle, the Druid, lived with his mother, Mémé, close to Uncle's house, maybe two miles away, and after my grandparents died the Druid and Mémé no longer saw any reason to visit Uncle, who lived holed up in his room, and that seemed to suit everyone, though they didn't completely lose contact: Mémé regularly called Uncle to announce that the Druid, her little boy, was lying dead at the foot of his bed—one day he'd choked on his own vomit, another it was his heart, his poor old heart that had given out just like that.

And whenever Mémé called Uncle climbed onto his hog, and we might picture him sighing and grumbling the way real rescuers do when they're called on a little too often, they always

have better things to do but they never refuse
to come to the aid of their uncles lying dead at
the foot of their beds, particularly because, according to Uncle, Mémé always called at the
worst possible time, when he was busy admir-
ing a duel between two seagulls or a hedgehog crossing through the yard next door, but
Uncle went anyway, just to be sure, and when
he reached Mémé's he paused outside his uncle's
bedroom, a basement room next to the heater
and the shelves stacked with canned food and
dog chow, and when Uncle got to the basement he first consulted his pendulum, because
Uncle never goes out without his pendulum, and
before he opened the door to the Druid's room
Uncle let his pendulum pendulate to see if the
Druid was dead, and he took his time consulting
his pendulum, and Mémé said for God's sake get
going, one way or another he's dead.

Mémé was the impatient sort, and she had
a little dog that was also the impatient sort, and
the dog growled and barked and headbutted
Uncle's leg, and it should be said that I never
thought that dog looked like a dog, it was blind
and hairless and there was something scaly about

its skin, and that animal reminded me more of some sea creature, a chimera from the depths of the Channel, probably picked up by Mémé in the bay after a particularly high tide, after which Mémé claimed that that glistening monster was a Yorkshire terrier, and of course no one would have dared contradict her, but anyway, Uncle refused to let himself be troubled by the thing gnawing at his calves, his eye was on the pendulum, and the pendulum said No to the left, and Uncle walked in and picked up the Druid, who'd passed out at the foot of his bed, as was his custom after the Vieille Auberge, and it must be said that passing out on the floor was a frequent event in the Druid's life, ever since he had to drink the health of the dead.

One day the pendulum swung to the right, and that day the Druid really was dead at the foot of his bed, and Uncle never fails to observe that it was only to be expected, and that day Uncle picked up his uncle, hoisted him over his shoulder like a potato sack, a potato sack with only one or two potatoes in it, because apparently the Druid weighed next to nothing, and Mémé's strange, voracious creature had already been at work on the carcass, says Uncle, and evidently Mémé was openly relieved, and afterward, in the retirement home, she boasted that she'd outlived both her sons.

6

There's a short story by Kafka that I like a lot because it reminds me of the village supermarket, a very short story called "The Cares of a Family Man," about an indefinable creature named Odradek, a creature the narrator compares to a sort of flat spool of thread, which for no reason invites itself into the home of a good family of Prague, and that good family of Prague struggles to discover some purpose to it, but the creature, which as it happens is endowed with the power of speech, is forever clouding the question of its function and the reason for its visit, and I find that story very beautiful because it reminds me of the village supermarket, where Odradeks are legion, especially in the bargain aisle, and like in Kafka's story you can certainly try to describe those things in the bargain aisle, but no matter how you study them, handle them, sniff them, examine them from every angle, there's always a trace of the unknown, a cog, a hiss, a mysterious thing you run up against, something that stops you short.

What can't be denied is that those objects cost so little a person could easily buy several, maybe hundreds, just in case, as a backup, and if you think no one buys that sort of Kafkaesque merchandise you're mistaken: Uncle, for instance, is a fan of those bargain-aisle Odradeks, which he calls fantastic, wonderful, extraordinary, not making it clear if it's their use or their appearance he admires, almost certainly both. Here, for informational purposes, is a short list of the Odradeks acquired more or less recently by Uncle: a toothpick-case in the form of a mussel smoking a cigarette; a crumb collector with tiny tractor wheels; a cellphone holder in the form of a humanoid crêpe with outstretched arms; a cup embellished with an extremely blurry photo of cats licking each other; a pack of emotional sponges (with the happy sponge, the silly sponge, the sad sponge, the smitten sponge); a timer in the form of a ladybug; a timer in the form of Groucho Marx glasses; a transparent false egg to be boiled in the pot along with the real eggs, where it turns first green, then blue, then purple, which has some vague connection to the doneness of the real eggs; and of course the celebrated sausage guillotine in its box graced with the portraits of Danton and Robespierre.

Uncle is always dazzled by the wealth of items on offer in the bargain aisle, and he thinks about his nephew who has a birthday soon and who's interested in the French revolution, and he thinks about his sister the cat-lover, and about his niece too, and just so no one will get jealous, Uncle decides to become the proud owner of a certain number of those trinkets, just in case, as backup, and anyway you never need a reason to give someone a present.

Uncle lives mostly in his room, where there's a big window through the mansard roof, and through that window Uncle has a view of the mole-hill-swollen yard, and the stables, and part of the bay, and at the beginning of spring, when Uncle starts to get hot up in his lair and the horses start grazing on the other side of the hedge, Uncle unsheathes his electrified tennis racket to massacre the flies, because the more horses there are the more flies there are, and those flies are big biting flies that land everywhere—on horses and other living things—and Uncle says they feed on the blood of the mammals they parasitize, and they multiply while they're at it, they multiply, says Uncle, arming himself with a second tennis racket and without even leaving his bed, a racket in each hand, Uncle commits the first fly murders of the spring.

It was when his parents died that Uncle developed that mania for holing up in his room, supposedly to watch over the house, a guard-dog duty assigned to him, according to family legend, by his dying father: You'll watch over the house, my son, the painter of naked women on the beach is supposed to have said as he lay dying of terminal cirrhosis: You'll close the shutters, the curtains, and you'll live locked up in your room, but sometimes you'll cut the grass, it's very important to keep the grass cut, there's nothing finer than a neatly trimmed lawn, and you'll see to it that no one comes after my dusty old bric-a-brac, because that's your inheritance, your treasure.

Uncle follows his papa's instructions to the letter, and when he's alone he listens for the creaking floorboards and anomalous breathing that might betray a malevolent presence, and Uncle has a baseball bat that he always keeps near his bed, with other weapons that he's very obviously never had to use, since according to him most of the unexpected slamming doors, murmurs, and footsteps are attributable to ghosts, and Uncle's not scared of ghosts, on the contrary, he loves them, he listens to them, he watches them, and he says hello to them as they go by.

It's true that the house creaks and cracks, and on a very windy day you might even think you hear voices up in the attic, and while I haven't yet had the good fortune to meet up with any ghosts here, I don't entirely rule out the possibility of some night coming face to face with my grandmother in her evening gown, lipstick crushed against her teeth, her skin a little waxier than when she was alive, but it's not those presences that haunt Uncle in the strictest sense of the word—Uncle is inhabited by other spirits that he regularly invokes, mischievous spirits he likes to imitate, unless those imitations are them possessing him: to mimic the Baron Uncle puts on a shrill voice, a voice without vocal cords, tracheotomized, miraculously preserved, and to mimic Caniche Uncle sucks in his cheeks and hunches his back, and for Chouquette Uncle literally crawls on the tile dining-room floor, and for Jessy, the rebel who committed suicide, Uncle spews torrents of insults and sputum at everyone around him, and the climax of the show is his improbable imitation of the Druid, a challenge if ever there was one, which Uncle meets with the greatest of ease, stretching out his garden-gnome physique to the dimensions of a hunched old man, as gnarled as an aged, storm-wracked tree.

There's one imitation Uncle is particularly proud of, his crowning achievement, or at least the one that demanded the most from him, because to mimic his father who suffered from an, alas, non-congenital malformation Uncle had to subject himself to unnatural stress positions, feet out, heels together, a ballerina in first position, and after many years his dogged efforts ended up paying off, because now Uncle is stuck with the waddle that so hobbles his walk, and as a reward his performance earned him a pair of yellow crutches and a metal plate in his hip.

Animals can't read, and in my brother's and my opinion the work we do serves no purpose, because what we do is translate packaging and catalog descriptions of products intended for animals of all stripes, instructions and descriptions that will never be read by the consumer, the animal, which will thus find itself forced into consuming certain products by our translations' true addressee, its master, who will choose everything according to his own tastes, and his habitat, and the color of his curtains or his couch, and maybemore than anything else the color of his pet.

The online catalog of the pet supply site we work for is a bottomless pit, a vertiginous list of merchandise, updated every day, a perpetually expanding ocean, and that immensity exists because the pet supply site aspires to meet every demand, and because the pet supply site strives to leave no choice to chance, and so you will find your heart's desire if your heart's desire is to chew a rubber sausage, or if you like nothing better than running after a pompom attached to a fishing pole, unless you'd rather rub against a natural-sisal post while eating heart-shaped semi-moist kibble in a spruce-wood cabin, and you can abandon yourself to those delights with perfect safety thanks to the reflective vests and life jackets available in all sorts of sizes, and there are wool caps for wintertime, and there are remote-control cat flaps, and there are retractable leashes and extendable leashes, leashes with fluorescent harnesses, and anti-tick shampoo and anti-lice shampoo, vitamin tablets, and digestive food supplements, and there are multicolored poo bags and plastic water toys that you put in the freezer, and there are treats made from maggots and red mosquito larvae, and the canned salmon is truly delicious, and that's the work my brother and I do, eight hours a day, sitting at our computers, and it's like drowning every day in the depths of an aquarium.

My brother's been working for the pet supply site for four years now, and I've been at it for two, and my brother often cautions me, and he tells me you have to watch out for the catalog, for the quasi-magnetic attraction it ends up exerting on the employee, and he tells me to beware of the treats that promote good oral hygiene, the rubber balls, the scratching pads, the soothing hemp-oil drops, and my brother says you've got to be wary, because all the real rodents, hamsters, rabbits, gerbils, and rats also exist in the form of adorable and very soft stuffed animals, and my brother tells me that most of all you have to take care not to get caught up in the catalog's diabolical spiral, and he tells me it's a fine line, and easily crossed, and he himself, two years ago, used the employee discount we enjoy to acquire a set of stress balls that have accompanied him ever since wherever he goes.

Uncle started work at the abbey twenty-three years ago, and he remembers the exact date he assumed his post as a gardener/landscaper, the eighth of August 1997, a Friday, strangely, and Uncle was thirty years old, and one day whose exact date no one remembers—I imagine it was also a Friday, the end of a week that was a little busier than the others—Uncle had to change jobs, but no one knows if that forced conversion was a promotion or a step down, in any case Uncle found himself assigned to peeling vegetables, veg prep man, he says, not seeming to question the conditions of his new work, and I'd find it very hard to say if Uncle enjoys being a veg prep man, which like every other sort of change he seems to accept, but in any case, and in the opinion of his doctors, he's better off sitting on a stool with a paring knife than he was hoisting a hoe, bending and swooping over the hydrangeas, which was how he had his first attack, one summer Friday.

Regularly my mother used to ask us how to calculate the age of a cat, I mean the age of a cat
in human age, since apparently feline age in itself doesn't count, and my mother could never
manage to remember that sort of thing, and she
was never sure if you were supposed to add two
years every year or three years every four years,
and in the end she would call us up on that pretext alone, arguing that we were well situated to
remind her of things like that when she forgot
them, and it's true, after all, we're translators, and
isn't that calculation a sort of translation?

On the pet supply site it says a cat hits the
age of human adulthood, which according to
our employer is eighteen years old, when it's six
months old, but wouldn't it be better to write
"after six months of life," and it also says you
have to wait two years to see your cat reach the
age of a young man, which is to say twenty-four
according to our employer, and once that grim
milestone is passed the cat will start to go downhill at great speed, and you can add four years
with every passing year, and we told our mother
that and she pretended she was suddenly remembering it, and in her defense I have to say

that her questions were far from idle, because all her life my mother has been the owner of several cats, some of which, by my estimates, were more than a hundred (human) years old.

Uncle's been all sorts of ages, and now he's fifty-two, and not long ago Uncle lost an incisor which he claims had been wobbling for a while before it suddenly fell out, and my mother doesn't think it's normal for her brother to be losing his incisors from one day to the next, and in my opinion it's inaesthetic more than anything else, because this way Uncle looks like a derelict, like a sort of vagrant from the Middle Ages, but Uncle's no stickler for aesthetics, he says it's all just a question of habit: going to work, peeling potatoes all day long, having an iron plate in your hip, living alone, you get used to it.

The first time we visited Uncle's vegetable garden there were already no more nuns at the abbey, evidently a consequence of that establishment's progressive secularization, it was something like a sanatorium and a community center rolled into one, and all the nuns my mother used to know and used to tell us about—her half-imaginary descriptions rooted in the cliché of the sassy, irrepressible nun—had either died or were in death's waiting room, the hospice at Immaculate Conception, a convent with a palliative care ward, where the sisters were transferred when they were nearing the finish line, the ones who were sick or too old, the ones who no longer had the strength to welcome ecumenical congregations and conferences on macrobiotics, or keep the books, or stand up, and contrary to my mother's claims, Uncle never cared much for the sisters, he even seemed not to trust them, their honeyed smiles and their old-candle complexions, their feigned old-maid kindliness, but none of that mattered now, because now Erwan had taken over, and the first time we visited the garden Uncle was eager to introduce Erwan, and Uncle had been telling us about Erwan for a long time, and Erwan was off in a corner of the garden with two other men who, we learned, were also named Erwan, and we thought the same thing, my mother, my brother, and me, we thought that three Erwans isn't something you see every day, and we greeted them as if they were strange animals, and they didn't trouble to introduce themselves, probably because they were tired of that little routine.

One of the Erwans explained to us that without Uncle the guests wouldn't have any vegetables to eat, and Uncle smiled and it seemed like he might have been flattered, and Erwan was wearing green shorts and he had scratches on his legs, no doubt from his many battles with the brambles, and the other Erwan was in charge of cutting and clearing, which is to say anything involving lawn mowers, brambles, and ivies, and the second Erwan, who was shorter and had a red beard, had been biting his nails ever since we came along and never stepped away from his bean basket, and the third Erwan, the head gardener, told us that he lived not far from the abbey in a little trailer all by himself and traveled three times a year to Nepal for his association, then he told us that he also had a garden, and for a while now he'd been keeping a yak in his garden, and the other

Erwan interrupted Erwan to say that if Erwan could look after a yak it was because he didn't have a family, and he said that in the tone of a gentle joke that meant no harm to anyone, and the three Erwans began to chuckle, and it was a comradely chuckle, the kind you only share with good fellow workers, and it was so nice to see them all laughing together, so we laughed too, my brother, my mother, and I, and Uncle wasn't really laughing, he hadn't been following the conversation, because he wanted to show my mother the squash seedlings he'd told her about before, and he was impatient, and he was waiting for us to stop laughing so he could show her the squash seedlings, and I myself would gladly have heard a bit more about that yak, but my mother insisted on being told how many beans were in the basket next to Erwan, and Erwan very quickly told her that there were over twenty pounds of beans in the basket, and he lifted the basket and made a face like he was exhausted because the basket was very heavy, and Uncle said that the squash seedlings were off this way at the end of the row and we said Let's go see, and Erwan with his bean basket was the only one who didn't say goodbye to us, because he'd gotten distracted, and because he was discreetly waving one hand in the air, because for some time he'd been trying to shoo away a fly that kept landing on his cheek.

We headed toward the squash seedlings, and the seedlings already had yellow flowers, and my brother thought the flowers were very beautiful, so it was with those three good-hearted men that Uncle spent his days at the abbey, I told myself, and my brother thought they seemed like a good team, Erwan, Erwan, Erwan, and Uncle, and they also seemed to have a fondness for Uncle, did Erwan, Erwan, and Erwan, and lunch at the abbey always ended with my mother saying In any case you're in very good hands here, and Uncle just said Yes, he was getting impatient because it was already three o'clock, and at three o'clock Uncle's workday is done, and we left the abbey at the same time as him, us in a car, him on his moped.

My brother, who was struggling with his Spanish lessons, one day needed help ordering a bouquet of flowers, the bouquet being a surprise for his little ladyfriend, a thought from afar, and I'm not sure I completely understood his calculations, but apparently the number of flowers in the bouquet referred to the date they met, and my brother also wanted my thoughts about the flowers—their colors, their scents—because he believed his friend preferred discreet flowers, wildflowers, like me apparently, and he also needed a hand to come up with the sweet little note in Spanish, and fortunately for my brother I didn't have a little ladyfriend, which meant I could devote my attention to his.

Several times I've asked Uncle if he's ever been in love, and every time he's told me about a certain Karine, a thing that went back to preschool, and that's more or less all I know about it, but on the other hand I do know that several times Uncle visited the clubs of Pigalle in the company of his friend Manu, and on that score I remember some not-particularly-glorious anecdotes involving surly sidewalk touts, stories where Uncle never got what he'd paid for, but deep down I don't think he cared that much about ogling the dancing women, because it was Manu who was leading him into it, and I think Uncle has never been sexually attracted to anyone or anything, but my brother says of course he has, that's the only way it can be, but I wouldn't be so categorical, because after all Uncle lives in a harem, in the middle of naked odalisques lounging on the beach, in his father's paintings, and they don't seem to have any effect on him.

One day I was sitting in the living room reading, and when Uncle came home from work he went into the kitchen, and he put what he'd bought in the refrigerator, and he said it had been a hot day, hotter than usual, and they were saying there'd be rain tomorrow, then he stopped halfway up the stairs and he said it was weird, another vegetable cleaner, Catherine, was always talking to him, and I asked if this Catherine was a nice woman and Uncle answered yes, a very nice woman, and since Uncle was still standing glued to the spot halfway up the staircase, I asked him to tell me a little more about her, and Uncle confided that Catherine was about five feet five inches tall, like me apparently, only much fatter, and she had chestnut hair, and a diamond in her nose, and she was very fond of crime novels, then I told him I thought this Catherine sounded very nice and she was probably trying to seduce him while they cleaned vegetables, and Uncle seemed very pleased to hear that, as if it confirmed a suspicion of his and now he didn't need to talk anymore, he went on upstairs, and I realized that this was the first time I'd talked about love with Uncle, and I think I remember that that April afternoon I was reading *My Friends*, by Emmanuel Bove, a book that tells the sad story of Victor Bâton, a war invalid who wants nothing so much as a friend to escape his solitude, and I never heard any mention of Catherine again, but I enthusiastically recommend Emmanuel Bove's *My Friends*.

7

When she was twenty my mother left France to live in Switzerland, which is where my brother and I were born, and where we grew up, in an old house on the side of a mountain, and it was in that house that our father gave us two rabbits we kept in a hutch, and it was in that house that one summer day, following an unnamable scent, I came across three corpses, and for a long time my mother told us the rabbits had been eaten by a fox, which didn't fool us, and I still can't understand why my father thought he had to sacrifice the rabbits before turning to himself.

My mother doesn't particularly like talking about those rabbits, she'd rather talk about our childhood Christmas tree, which is a tiny plastic folding tree that we still get out for the holidays, and just like a real tree my mother's tree is losing branches and not much is left of its 1970s splendor, and my mother and Uncle still refuse to throw the thing away even as it sheds its needles and sags a little more each year under the weight of the decorations and last Christmas Uncle even bought a new star to replace the original, which had become nothing but rusted iron wire, and it's always been Uncle who puts the star at the top of the tree, because apparently it's the youngest child's job to put the star at the top of the tree.

Uncle was fifteen when my mother moved to Switzerland, and he was doing a horticulture apprenticeship at the Château d'Arnouville, not far from Montmagny, and I saw in an old brochure stuck in Uncle's papers that it started out as a horticultural training center for shell-shocked World War I veterans, and with the dwindling of that—to say the least—very specific customer base I can see why the school had to diversify, and Uncle says there were all sorts at the Château d'Arnouville: some were ex-cons, some had a mental or physical handicap, and some were schizophrenic, and the brochure called those ones "adolescents with behavioral challenges," though Uncle, who seems to have got his certificate without too much trouble, prefers to call them "a real bunch of jokers."

Last Christmas my mother wasn't sleeping well, she woke up shrieking in the middle of the night, because as it happens one of her two cats had died, and just after it died my mother drove off, twelve hours on the road from Switzerland to Brittany, sobbing all the way, not to mention that it was freezing cold, and at night my mother was haunted by her dreams, and during the day she said over and over that the first thing to do was apply for the certificate of compliance so she could legally register the car in France, the car she'd driven all the way here, something had to be done with that thing, she said, and she started to cry again, hard, and one time it was because of the cat and the next it was because she didn't know where to go for the certificate of compliance, and that said, the more my mother focused on paperwork the better she slept.

One evening my mother was lying in her bed in the attic when she smelled a strange smell, a smell my mother said came from her brother's room, and she told us she wanted to have a look in Uncle's room, and my brother and I were surprised, because we would never have dared imagine that one day we would go into Uncle's room, where as children we were convinced Uncle had all kinds of wonderful stuff, but my mother would only say there was a bad smell upstairs and it wasn't the workshop's worm-eaten beams or damp walls, and she insisted on going into her brother's room to look around, and since I'd come to know that sort of worry very well in the wake of my rabbits' death, the next day we waited for Uncle to go off on his usual trip to the supermarket, and just to be sure we'd have enough time my mother gave Uncle a slightly complicated shopping list: olive oil, potatoes, black soap, baking soda, non-fluoride toothpaste, enough to keep him wandering the supermarket aisles for an hour, easily.

There's a step outside the door to Uncle's room, and my mother almost tripped because she hadn't walked through that doorway for almost twenty years, and when she looked up my mother blurted out Oh how horrible! and my brother didn't answer, his eyes were glistening and my mother said again Oh how horrible! and I wanted to turn around and leave, and again my mother said Oh how horrible and I stood on the step in the cloud of dust my mother had raised when she stumbled, and I looked hard at my brother's eyes and Uncle's room.

There was a holey foam mattress on the floor, and at least fifty tote bags from the supermarket, and newspapers and TV guides, and archery magazines and Coke bottles and beer cans, and wrappers from cookies or chocolate cakes, and toys, knives, fake pistols, books, records, and there were strands of black dust hanging from the ceiling, and there were spiderwebs, and ashtrays invisible beneath mountains of cigarette butts spilling onto the grime-crusted nightstand, and next to the nightstand was a pair of crutches, and there were no sheets on the bed, and no box spring under the bed, only that holey, stained foam mattress, and near the ironically empty plastic wastebasket there were maybe ten beer bottles full of urine, and those bottles were lined up and the liquid was a little foamy in the necks, and although we'd supposed Uncle was kind of a slob we never expected to find such a dump, and my mother said again and again Oh how horrible Oh how horrible and I know my brother quickly runs out of patience when my mother gets stuck like that, and maybe that's why he started picking things up, among them a chicken bone that he stuffed into his pocket for lack of a better place or because he was getting madder and madder, and meanwhile I was eyeing the room and scrutinizing the garbage and taking deep breaths of that nauseating smell of cigarette butts and dust and urine, the most nauseating smell I've ever taken deep breaths of, I think.

Trembling, my mother went to the roof window and hopped a few times in hopes of opening it, and for a while she hopped in vain, but eventually she got ahold of the bar and opened the window, then looked at her hand and said Oh how horrible because her hand was black with filth and I was expecting to find dead mice and cockroaches in the armoire among my uncle's underwear, some of which, given the size, must have come from when he was five years old, and I was expecting to find a bunch of spiders that had taken advantage of this vacuum-free zone to build the biggest web in the history of spiders, but my brother said no lifeform could have survived in that room, not a single one, except Uncle.

That year Uncle didn't set up the Christmas tree as he usually did, because after that little tour of his bedroom no one was in the mood to get out the tree, and on Christmas Eve my brother just made spaghetti, and at the dinner table Uncle, who hadn't said a word since he sat down, was pale and drawn, and that was strange because Uncle loves spaghetti, but now he was breathing loudly over his plate, and he seemed like he'd sunk into a deep emptiness, and he struggled to suck down the long noodles, and my mother, my brother, and I stared at Uncle's hands, because his hands were swollen and blue, and we gave each other questioning glances, until my mother broke the silence and said You know we looked in your room, and You know that's not normal, and You know after all you're not a pig, and You know I'm ashamed, and It's so filthy and Look how swollen and blue your hands are, Do you think that's normal, tell me, she asked Uncle, but Uncle didn't react, even though he couldn't not have heard what his sister was saying, and I wonder if he felt betrayed or ashamed that Christmas Eve, and if he hated us without enough breath in him to yell at us, or enough strength to put an arrow in his bow and dispatch the three of us then and there.

Faced with my uncle's silence my mother couldn't keep from crying, and she tried to change the subject, and she started talking about the certificate of compliance that we had to request as soon as possible and the terrine of wild boar she'd eaten with our neighbors Monsieur and Madame Charrieau, and then, faced with everyone's silence, my mother lost her temper and pounded her fists on the table and said she couldn't even talk about meat with my brother and me around because my brother and I didn't eat meat, and we didn't react, our eyes were on Uncle, who got up to run to the toilet and as a rule my mother hated it when her brother left the table to go to the toilet in the middle of the meal, and she exclaimed What, he can't hold it? and she sighed, and she rolled her eyes, and her eyes glistened and rolled at the same time, but what she didn't understand was that if her brother didn't go to the bathroom immediately he would wet himself, like a cloudburst, like a rainstorm no one had forecast.

The next day my mother packed her suitcase to go back to Switzerland, where her work was waiting and her second cat too, the one that was still alive, not the other one, but this one had the same problem, a thyroid problem, and he wouldn't eat, and to make him gain weight and not die my mother had to put a radioactive iodine-based cream in his ears and since the cream was very toxic to human beings my mother had to wear gloves every time she applied it, and that was the very first thing she did when she came home from work, even before she took off her shoes, she went looking for the cat to cream his ears, and when the cat wasn't there my mother got worried, because he was a cat who was afraid of lightning, and he was afraid of rain and lawn mowers, and because he was a hard cat to catch, my mother would wait hours in the yard, radioactive cream at the ready, for the cat to show the tips of his ears.

Before she left my mother seemed agitated, she went upstairs to say goodbye to her brother, but Uncle was still sleeping, and my mother didn't want to wake him just to say goodbye, and she paced around, and she kept clearing her throat, hoping there would be a train for her to take in spite of the strike, because there was a big strike going on at the time, and my mother had got unused to strikes, because there are never strikes in Switzerland, and just before she left the house she even thought she'd lost her train ticket, so things got frantic for a minute and my brother and I looked around the living room for the train ticket, but the ticket was in her document organizer, where my mother organizes all her documents, and to hear her talking and fussing you might have thought she was deathly afraid of her suitcase and her document organizer and her ticket and the strike, and my mother made a theatrical sad face, turning down the corners of her mouth, and she explained her side of things: You know, she told us, I didn't leave home when I was twenty just to come back thirty-five years later and live with my brother and change his diapers, and she asked if we could understand that, and she looked at me and said: How would you like having to change your brother's diapers, and my brother laughed and he said we understood, and I didn't answer her because my brother had said we understood.

8

First thing, the village doctor took Uncle's blood pressure with the inflatable armband, and I know Uncle can't stand being touched, but Uncle didn't complain, and the doctor listened to Uncle's heart with a stethoscope and looked at his hands, then his ankles, which were also swollen and blue, which we hadn't noticed before because Uncle never goes barefoot, and he always tucks his cuffs into his socks because his pants are always too long for his short, asymmetrical legs, and the doctor pushed up the cuffs and pressed on Uncle's feet with his index finger, and finally, in a flat voice that didn't go with the news, he said Uncle's case was extremely urgent, and I think that was the first time I'd ever laid eyes on that pair of flat feet with long, dirty nails, and according to the doctor Uncle's blood pressure was way too high, but Uncle said that was normal because he didn't like doctors, or dentists, and he said his blood pressure was always way too high when he went to see them, but the doctor made it clear that we weren't supposed to listen to him, and we had to hurry, because our uncle's life was in danger, and my brother and I asked the doctor where we should go, and the doctor sent us to a specialist in uncles.

The specialist in uncles had an office in a hospital I'd never heard of, but Uncle knew it well because he'd taken the Druid there, he recognized the parking lot on the hill, and he was talking in a very shrill voice, a heavy-metal voice that in Uncle's case was the voice of fear, and according to Monsieur and Madame Charrieau that hospital didn't exactly inspire confidence, it should have been shut down long before because of the antiquated equipment and the lack of staff and certain doctors who deserved to be hauled before a judge, but we didn't have a choice, and we parked the car just by the revolving door at the hospital entrance and for a moment we eyed the massive block of dull-gray concrete from which, in spite of the rumors, a great crowd of people were streaming.

And some of those people on their way out of the hospital had cats or dogs on leashes, and others were pressing Guinea pigs or ferrets to their breasts, and the Guinea pigs were squeaking anxiously, as if they'd just gone through a rough time, and still others had budgies in cages and a woman in a wheelchair was carrying a parrot on her right arm, and we observed that fauna in silence for ten full minutes before my brother made up his mind to ask if we were sure we were in the right place, and Uncle said Yes yes, he knew this hospital well, he'd taken his uncle the Druid there three or four times before he died at the foot of his bed, but Uncle's answer was drowned out by a bellow, and when I say bellow I'm thinking for example of the sound a cow makes on the way to the slaughterhouse, and my brother and I could scarcely believe what we were seeing, and it must be said that it's not every day you see a huge long-haired bovine coming out of a hospital in Brittany, and Uncle didn't seem to think anything of it and said it was a yak, and we remembered Erwan's yak and we asked Uncle if that beast was Erwan's yak but Uncle said No no, this one was a young yak, you could tell by its coat, and besides it was scarcely six feet long, and we were so surprised by Uncle's expert answer that we said nothing more, and the yak's young owner gave a sharp tug on the halter to extract the animal, which was caught in the revolving door, and Uncle had a coughing fit in the car, and as he coughed he spit on his sweater, yellow mucus faintly streaked with blood, I think, and I said to my brother Let's go and we got out of the car and we stopped at the revolving door where the yak's monumental, hairy, muscular mass suddenly got free, clearing the way for the other patients, and the other patients streamed out under the covered entryway, patients in bad shape, patients in rough condition, missing a piece of head, arm, or lung, patients with crutches and patients with bandages, patients with the gray skin of smokers who live in a rainy climate, patients like Uncle.

The waiting room had the usual hospital smell mixed with canned cat food and sheep suint, and maybe also cow dung, and we sat down on chairs facing the front desk where a young man was giving directions to patients, and on the waiting-room walls there were posters about nutrition and blood pressure, injections, suppositories, and the national health system, and my brother carefully studied the posters in the waiting room: heart rates and health campaigns encouraging everyone to eat meat every day, three times a day, as often as possible, for their health's sake, and my brother got annoyed and scratched at his head, No surprise, he said, if this is the kind of stuff they put up in waiting rooms, and Uncle was staring at the front desk as if he could control the young man's every move with his eyes or as if he were sitting in a movie theater waiting for the film to come on, but maybe he was just waiting for something to happen, waiting to be sent home, to be given good news, and my eyelids itched with exhaustion and allergies to mammal hair, all mammal hair, and after something like a half hour the young man called us, and my brother stood up first, and he told Uncle to get up too, and we followed the young man to a little room where he gestured to us to sit down on two chairs, and when the doctor came in he discovered there were three of us and he begged our pardon and went off for a stool, and my brother took the stool and I took one of the two chairs, and we sat down a little ways away, my brother and I, so the doctor could examine Uncle properly.

The doctor wanted to know who we were, in relation to Uncle I mean, and Uncle pointed at us and said She's my niece and he's my nephew, and the doctor squinted at us like someone contemplating a menhir in the mist, and he listened to Uncle's heart and immediately began to ask questions even as he continued the examination, which is to say as he touched Uncle's ankles and neck more or less as firmly as the village doctor, and he asked us: how old is he, does he live alone, does he drink, does he eat a lot, what about meat, stools, exercise, sleep, how many hours a day does he spend lying down, social behavior, responsiveness, obedience, thyroid, oral hygiene, calcium, potassium, magnesium, zinc, and my brother and I tried to answer most of his questions like this was a lightning round in a quiz show, and when we didn't know the answer we shrugged, and there was a lot we didn't know about Uncle's life, and whenever we didn't have an answer Uncle raised his hand and breathlessly tried to explain that he just had a little cold, which was perfectly normal, after all it was flu season, no cause for alarm.

Then the doctor told us Uncle had water in his lungs and toxins in his blood, and he said nothing was working right in Uncle's body, not his kidneys, not his liver, not his heart, and the doctor explained that Uncle didn't just have a cold, he'd had a pulmonary embolism, and according to the doctor Uncle had to stay in the hospital if we wanted to keep him alive, and I thought of the anatomy book we studied in high school, which I still sometimes looked through in the evening because that book showed everything so prettily, the liver and the spleen and the gaily colored intestines, like magnolia and hydrangea flowers, and I thought about those beauteous bowels and I supposed Uncle's insides were very different, dark, undoubtedly boggy, with a stream flowing between his coal-black lungs amid a gray, cracked-up landscape, and here and there it burned, it throbbed, wherever the blood couldn't circulate properly, wherever the arteries were plugged up as if by dams of dead wood.

They put Uncle on a gurney and the doctor called a nurse to take him to the fifth floor, the pulmonology ward, and Uncle lay on the gurney looking at the ceiling, and he had his hands clasped on his fat stomach like a little boy, or like a corpse bound for the morgue, and the leather cord of his pendulum hung from his balled hands, and the pendulum was all Uncle had brought with him, and I don't know if that's because he thought he'd go home that evening thanks to the pendulum or if the pendulum was the one thing he couldn't do without. We looked at Uncle on the gurney and we found it hard to believe he was in danger of dying that night, because he was wiggling his holey old tennis shoes on the gurney and lifting his head to see over his stomach and make sure we were following him, and the nurse pushing the gurney stopped in the middle of the hallway and put the brake on with her foot, and she asked us to wait, and we went

to Uncle, and I looked at Uncle who wasn't exactly acting like a dying man, and he said This
place is nuts, and he was laughing, and there
were noises in the hallway, cries and moans, and
we could tell Uncle was afraid, and my brother
leaned over him and he said Don't be afraid, and
Uncle said No no I'm fine, and we knew he was
lying, and when the nurse came back to tell us
they'd found a room we gave Uncle a hug and
promised to come back the next day, and we left
the hospital, and the night was deep and dark
and it was raining, there was no one left in the
parking lot, and in the car on the way home we
told each other this would be the first time we'd
ever slept in the house without Uncle.

The next day my brother and I decided to take
the opportunity to clean Uncle's room, and the
task was so daunting that we first thought of
throwing everything out the window, making a
pile of it all in the yard and burning it all in a
big bonfire, but we soon thought better of that,

realizing it would be the same as incinerating Uncle's whole life, and then my brother and I went to the home center next to the supermarket, and we bought gloves and masks and white suits that looked like something the liquidators of a nuclear power plant would wear, and we went back to the house and we called Uncle at the hospital to find out how his first night had gone and also to ask permission to clean his room, and Uncle told us the nurses had drained the juice out of him, more than two gallons in a single night apparently, and Uncle said it was OK about his room as long as we didn't throw anything out the window.

In the very back of Uncle's armoire my brother discovered a leather briefcase with a thick layer of dust on it, and in that leather briefcase was a collection of bank statements from the past thirty years, and diplomas from his horticulture school, and evaluations from psychologists and doctors, and school reports that always reported the same thing— mediocre hygiene, little capacity for group work—and also in the briefcase were the results of a mammogram they gave Uncle when he was little, and we found that strange and fascinating, and until we realized it was just a little excess of estrogen we imagined our uncle might have been born a woman, then we closed the briefcase and cleared all the shelves and cabinets and sorted through Uncle's things, books, records, toys, and we stacked them up without paying much attention to them, and we took all the furniture out of the workshop, and we scrubbed the floor with black soap, and with every swipe of the sponge the original orange of the linoleum reappeared, and it was almost a pleasure to clean something that dirty, and my brother took one half of the floor and I took the other, and we had to go and get knives to scrape away the filth that in some places had been accumulating for thirty years, and then we put all the furniture back, and the operation took about eight hours, and our liquidation suits were rumpled and worn through, and at the end of the day we didn't have the strength to go to the hospital and visit Uncle.

That evening my brother set his computer on the kitchen table between two plates of pasta and randomly clicked on a travel documentary, and it turned out to be a documentary about Switzerland, and we knew all about Switzerland since we were born there and we'd spent most of our lives there, and maybe we weren't in the mood for exoticism that night, and maybe we even thought it would be nice to dream of Switzerland for a while, unless we were just too exhausted to change the video, in any case we watched the documentary about Switzerland, and the documentary about Switzerland started in the mountains of the Valais, which the announcer pompously called the Nepal of Europe, and we followed a group of local hikers dressed in the finest technical gear and top-quality walking shoes, shoes that have nothing in common with the walking shoes bought and worn by mere mortals, no, the Swiss wear shoes that grip the mountainside, veritable masterpieces of podiatric engineering, and among other things it's thanks to those aerospace-quality shoes that the Swiss can walk for days on narrow mountain paths overlooking unsoundable abysses, and my brother and I started to scratch and the camera flew away from the Valais and hovered over magnificent lakes of Swiss water, which is to say pure crystalline water, and the camera abruptly zoomed in on a cow that was grazing in a pasture, and it was a cow from the canton of Uri, and according to a cowherd by the name of Ueli, cows from the canton of Uri are the most beautiful cows in the world, and Ueli showed us his collection of rabbits, and my brother was scratching his neck and I was diligently scouring my eyelids, and our nails dug deep into our flesh, and Ueli's rabbits were very big, and several times Ueli had won the national competition for the biggest rabbit, and Ueli's wife came on to talk about her rounds of cheese, but we were scratching so hard that we didn't fully understand the milk coagulation process, and the camera, which was a Swiss army drone, flew away from Ueli and Sabine's rustic mountain home, and Sabine waved goodbye with one hand while with the other she cut into a round of cheese, and Ueli waved his left hand while his right hand clutched an enormous rabbit by the scruff of the neck, and little flakes of dead skin fell like snow on the oilcloth of the kitchen table and mingled with the parmesan on the untouched plates of pasta, and we were scratching ever more feverishly, and I think we'd both stopped pinning the blame on the dust we'd picked up during our day of cleaning, and it was Switzerland that was itching us till the blood flowed, and we couldn't look away, like we were hypnotized, and then came the list of Swiss records and statistics, and the Swiss records and statistics were triumphant, and Switzerland held in its snug, milky little bosom the best dentists and the best engineers and the best pilots and the best physicists and the best plastic surgeons and the best skiers, and Switzerland had logged the lowest percentage of dental abscesses in 2014, the lowest in the world of course, and a Swiss family's rows of white, impeccably tartar-free teeth appeared on the screen to illustrate that revelation and to show their uninflamed gums—mother, father, daughter, son, eight rows of impeccably white teeth tucked into tight, pale-pink gums—and the family seemed happy to have beautifully clean teeth, and who wouldn't be you may ask, and we were offered a quick panorama of the biggest little Swiss cities, and then the flying camera flew low over Lake Lucerne, where the Rütli Oath is commemorated every first of August, and the steel cables of the Schwyz-Stoos funicular, and the clouds at the tip of the Matterhorn, and the fog snaking through the mountains, those big mountains, those towering vertiginous peaks where women dance in traditional costumes, women who in some cantons of Switzerland were granted the right to vote in 1990, and the Swiss people were happy and they displayed their white crosses on a red background even in their neatly groomed yards, where three acne-riddled boys in uniform appeared, and the little soldiers said they were proud to serve their beautiful white cross on a red background and the little soldiers also said every little Swiss citizen would get their own little bunker in the event of a catastrophe, an invasion launched from Alsace, for example, or Burgundy, or the slightest tidal wave on Lac Leman, and my brother and I had moved on to the insides of our knees, a particularly delicate spot, easily shredded, and it was almost the end of the documentary, and the camera flew like a giant fly around a strange brown edifice, and it turned out that the thing was a Swiss chocolate fountain, a giant fountain, and this was the inauguration of the giant Swiss chocolate fountain, in the presence of the foremost Swiss CEOs, and the foremost Swiss singers and the foremost Swiss tennis players, and the tennis players plunged their rackets into the chocolate and the CEOs dipped their fingers in, and my brother and I were literally harrowing our flesh as we looked at those beautiful trickling Swiss images and all the invitees looked like Ueli and Sabine, as if Switzerland numbered only two inhabitants cloned into eight million copies, and the camera zoomed in on Ueli's smiling pink face, and then came the end credits, and without hesitating for a second my brother closed the laptop.

9

We went to see Uncle every day, and we always found Uncle sitting on his bed, because the doctors had forbidden him to stay lying down for too long, and as he sat Uncle looked at the TV hanging from the ceiling, and he was glad my brother had thought to buy him a TV subscription at the hospital kiosk, because this way it felt almost like being at home, and his stomach stuck out of his turquoise hospital shirt, and sometimes the nurse would come rushing in and lecture him: Really Monsieur, button your shirt, you have visitors, and that made Uncle laugh, and he explained to the nurse that we were his nephew and niece and his fat stomach wouldn't bother us, and we said No, it really didn't bother us, and the nurse waited for our confirmation, as if Uncle's words didn't count, and the nurse shook her head, You're sure, she said, as if she didn't trust any of us, and as soon as the nurse left the room Uncle told us of his deepest desires: apple juice and chocolate cookies, OK, we'll bring those next time, we said, and we always stayed maybe an hour, and the visits became a routine, Uncle's color was coming back, and one time on the way home my brother said there was no reason to make a big deal out of all this, now that we knew Uncle wasn't even going to die, no need to make a big drama out of it, because you can't write a drama or even a novel with just a few vague memories and hospital business, with the death of a rabbit or tales of a dilapidated inn, with an uncle who wasn't even dead, claimed my brother.

An Erwan from the abbey called us one evening to tell us we'd saved Uncle's life, but we didn't know which Erwan it was, and Erwan told us he was very concerned when he saw Uncle gasping and breathing heavily and getting worn out peeling carrots and stemming green beans, and Erwan told us the abbey didn't have our phone number, or our mother's in Switzerland, so there was no way he could have let us know, and Erwan even said that one day he'd suggested Uncle go see a doctor, and Uncle refused with a vehemence so unlike him that Erwan didn't dare bother him about it again, and he told us that lately it had been taking Uncle fifteen minutes to wash a head of lettuce, and no one wanted to work with him, lazy and worn-out as he was, and that was pretty much all Erwan told us that night, but since then Erwan has been calling regularly to ask how Uncle is doing.

Every morning my brother did online Spanish courses, and in the afternoon he turned to his fruit trees: he soaped them every day to keep the aphids away—he filled a cereal bowl with his soap mixture, and he dipped his index finger in the bowl and with his index finger he stroked every leaf—and my brother wiped his finger on a handkerchief then came running into the house to show me his handkerchief, and he said that was how they made colors for artists, and his handkerchief was all green, and it's true that it was a pretty green, and one day my brother deadheaded the hydrangeas, and that day there were dried-out hydrangea heads flying through the yard, and even out onto the road, and seeing all those hydrangea heads my brother got an urge to plant rose bushes, because flowers, he said, made him happy, it was just that simple but it wasn't that simple, and I understood what my brother meant, and with a touch of anxiousness in his voice my brother also said that he hoped his little ladyfriend would enjoy the bouquets he'd sent her, and he hoped to see his little ladyfriend again soon, and he started to daydream as he looked at the hydrangea corpses, telling himself that if he ever made any progress in Spanish he could move in with his little ladyfriend one day, but he didn't know when because it depended on her because she was still married, and their future, and the future in general, was hazy and uncertain, and

my brother asked me to stop calling his little
ladyfriend his little ladyfriend, and on his hospital bed Uncle often told us to take it easy on
the trees and flowers, because he was very fond
of the yard just as it was, flat, green, and surrounded by a tall hedge.

On his last day in the hospital Uncle went out
to wait for us in the hallway, in front of his
room, and he was restless, holding a plastic bag
full of dirty laundry in one hand, and he was
wearing his backpack on his back, and he gave a
start when he finally saw us coming, and he said
he'd been ready for hours, and he gave the bag
of dirty laundry to my brother, and the nurse
came along, and she quickly explained the routine we were supposed to follow: a dozen or so
pills to be downed every day before every meal,
absolutely no meat, no meat or sugar, but on
the other hand lots of walking, forty-five minutes of walking four times a week, and then,
about the anticoagulants, she said Uncle would

have to be very careful not to cut himself, And if you suddenly feel like you're gaining weight and turning blue call an ambulance, the nurse said to Uncle, the way you'd talk to a slightly backward child, then she gave us the discharge papers and we thanked her, and Uncle thanked her, very warmly, almost too, and he added that he'd had a wonderful stay, and the nurse pushed up her pink round glasses and we left the room, and Uncle was happy and he was waddling faster than usual, and we went to drop off the discharge papers at the front desk, and just before we left the hospital Uncle asked us to wait a few moments, because he really had to go to the bathroom.

When we got home Uncle made all sorts of promises, but we couldn't help closely surveilling him, although there was a big difference between my surveillance and my brother's, because I surveilled Uncle out of the corner of my eye, as discreetly as possible, whereas my brother was always breathing down Uncle's neck, and from time to time he knocked on his bedroom door to see if we was still vertical, and he fished the receipts out of Uncle's tote bags to see if he'd bought candy or alcohol, and fifty times a day he asked if he'd taken all his pills, which didn't stop him from counting the gelcaps and blister-packs and inspecting the boxes.

To keep Uncle from mixing up his pills I put stickers on the boxes, a yellow sticker for the morning pills, a green sticker for the mid-day pills, a red sticker for the evening pills, and in the evening Uncle has to take eight pills at once, first he takes them out one at a time, then he makes a little pile of them on the table, and then he lays the eight pills one by one on his tongue, and often he's talking at the same time, and when he's talking at the same time there's always at least one pill that falls out onto the table, and when that happens Uncle picks up the pill and puts it back on his tongue with the other pills, and then he stops talking, and he tries to keep them all balanced on his tongue, and gets himself a glass of water, then swallows his pills, and once the pills have been swallowed he says: That was a good dinner, and he goes up to his room to watch television.

My brother thought it was important for Uncle to go back to work as soon as he could, but the doctor extended his medical leave for another month, and every morning Uncle got up and ate his breakfast and went off to shoot arrows in the workshop, then he went out on his moped, and stopping by the supermarket and then by the bank to see how much he had left in his account, and one day Uncle came home with walkie-talkies, and we tried them out, and they worked up to more than three hundred meters, and from then on, when dinner was ready, we called Uncle by walkie-talkie.

My bedroom is across the hall from the toilet, and when we were little my brother and I shared that bedroom during vacations, and we shared it until the day we decided not to share it anymore, and that day my brother decided to split the garage in two and put up a partition wall, and at first Uncle took a dim view of that project, and he didn't approve of it at all because it took away half the garage from him and forced him to park his moped right by the lawnmower, but after many unsuccessful attempts Uncle ended up finding a way to slip his moped between the lawnmower and grandfather's old junk stored in the garage, and I got used to sleeping alone in the room across from the toilet.

Uncle was suffering severe nocturnal incontinence ever since he came home, and being a light sleeper I lay wide awake in my bed and listened to Uncle come down the stairs and open the door to the toilet room, and I heard him excreting and groaning, and sometimes it lasted more than an hour, and I don't know why, but at night Uncle always left the door to the toilet room open, and I didn't dare get up to ask him to close it, so I lay in my bed listening, and Uncle said Oh damn and Oh shit when he didn't make it in time, then he raced to the washroom and turned on the shower, then leaving the water on he went back to the toilet, talking to himself, saying things I couldn't understand because he was discreet enough to whisper, and it almost seemed like he was talking to someone, and after he flushed the toilet he went back to the washroom, still whispering, and he turned off the water, and he went to the kitchen, which is where the washing machine is, and I could still hear him groaning in front of the washing machine, probably because he had to bend over to set the cycle, and I could still tell what he was doing, in the kitchen he was putting his soiled underwear in the machine, and Uncle ran the machine for just one pair of soiled underwear, and when morning came there were still streaks and smears in the toilet bowl and on the seat and on the floor too, and my brother didn't hesitate to wake Uncle to order him to clean it up or wear adult diapers if there was something really wrong with him, but one time it was because of peanuts, and another time it was fruit juice, and Uncle went off to get a rag and some hot water to clean it all up as his nephew had asked.

My brother and his little ladyfriend had planned a trip to Italy, and my brother's little ladyfriend knew Italy well, and she promised to show him all around Rome in just four days, because she was a very busy little ladyfriend, who could only devote four days to Rome, which is why they arranged to meet in Switzerland, where they could easily get to Lombardy, then they would drive through the lake district in a rented car, stopping to eat ice cream in Como, and pizza on the shores of Lake Maggiore, and my brother told me his little ladyfriend had promised to show him the "typewriter," which is a Roman monument, and the ancient Pantheon, and the Fountain of the Turtles and the dome of Saint Peter's and all the marvels of Rome in four days.

And while my brother was eagerly looking forward to the Italian trip Uncle got a call from Erwan saying the abbey was going to close for a while, and it would be better if Uncle stayed home, and it would be better not to set off for any vacations in Italy, which is how we found ourselves stuck in the village, in our drafty old house, with Uncle, who was as happy as a king, and for Uncle that news was a miracle, a gift from heaven, and he went back to very slowly mowing the lawn, one little square yard of lawn every day, and I heard him talking with the neighbor, Monsieur Charrieau, who was also mowing his lawn, and they stood face to face with their lawn mowers like two baby strollers, and Uncle was talking very loudly and Monsieur Charrieau was too, because the lawn mowers were still running, and Uncle said to Monsieur Charrieau You see, we're all the same now, everyone's like me, and Monsieur Charrieau smiled in his big black sunglasses, but it was the smile of someone who didn't actually hear what the other person just said, probably because of the lawnmower, and because the Charrieaus' dog Mildiou had come running up barking, but that didn't trouble Uncle, he went back to his grass, and the neighbor to his, and Monsieur Charrieau gently kicked Mildiou away, and the dog had tousled gray fur, as if he'd been rolling in the mudflats, and the neighbor's grass was impeccably clipped and green, as if Monsieur Charrieau had hand-painted every blade.

My brother had passed his online Spanish test, almost a hundred percent, and he was proud of himself, in a good mood, and he mixed water and black soap in a pink spray bottle, and like every day he sprayed every leaf of each of his trees, starting with the cherry, and he said this way there wouldn't be any more aphids, and the ants would die and that was a shame but it had to be, and my brother called to Uncle, and he had to yell very loudly because it was afternoon and often in the afternoons Uncle slept in his room, but my brother wouldn't give up, and he went on calling to Uncle, and eventually Uncle stuck his head out the window and said What is it, curtly, sounding almost annoyed, and in a slightly more annoyed voice my brother answered Could you try to leave a little more grass around the fruit trees when you mow the lawn, I've told you before, they need lots of grass around them to grow, and Uncle said Yeah yeah, and Whatever, and he added that on TV they were saying the borders of countries were going to close, and my brother asked what borders exactly they meant, and Uncle said he didn't know, then he closed the window, and outside it was strangely warm for the beginning of spring, and I was sitting in a lawn chair, and my brother had tears in his eyes as he stood by his trees and went on spraying the leaves, the leaves of the quince tree and the persimmon tree, the leaves of the apple tree and the cherry tree, and now my brother knew he wouldn't be seeing his little ladyfriend anytime soon.

10

There was a storm one night, with winds up to eighty miles an hour, and my brother was in his room and I was in mine, and we both heard a big noise, and we rushed out of our rooms because we were worried about Uncle and we imagined he'd fallen or been crushed by some heavy object, and as we passed the window that looks onto the yard we saw the TV antenna lying on the ground, and we were relieved that it was the antenna and not Uncle that had fallen from the roof, and the antenna dated back to the seventies, and ever since that day it's been out in our yard, like a huge rusty rake, or a piece of a satellite fallen from the sky.

The day the antenna fell was also Uncle's birthday, and at lunchtime we called him by walkie-talkie, but the walkie-talkie's battery was dead, so my brother went to the bottom of the stairs and yelled Lunchtime, and Uncle yelled Coming, and he came downstairs and we sang Happy Birthday until he reached the last step, and my brother had made a dish of green lentils with carrots and bay leaves, and I'd made a chocolate mousse with two candles in it, one in the shape of a five and one in the shape of a three, and I lit the candles, then with my phone I took a picture of Uncle, and in the picture Uncle is holding his plate of lentils in front of his face and grimacing in disgust, and he wanted me to send the picture to his sister, because it would make her laugh, so I sent the picture to my mother and I advised Uncle to blow out the candles quickly, because the two candles were visibly sinking into the mousse, and Uncle got ready to blow and we told him to make a wish, and he wished out loud, and his wish was that he could soon go back to the supermarket, then Uncle blew very hard, and as he blew he spewed spit everywhere and my brother and I applauded.

The wind had damaged the leaves on the trees, and the leaves were all withered and torn, especially the ones on the apple tree, and my brother said that was very bad, because the apple was the pollinating tree, and along with the leaves the wind had broken branches, and he was also upset because his little ladyfriend had gotten the bouquet but hadn't understood the calculation, so my brother found himself forced to explain the surprise to his little ladyfriend, and it turned out that the florist had miscounted, and that idiot florist had put in two extra roses, and of course that way it was absolutely impossible for his little ladyfriend to understand the calculation, my brother said, and he threw his anti-stress dog ball at the ground, saying that in any case this whole thing was ridiculous, and he was sick of being here and Uncle not doing anything to help, and Uncle deliberately mowing right up to the trees, and he never aired out his room, and he never changed his sheets, and he ate way too many chocolate cookies, and he never got any exercise, and he washed even less than he used to, and my brother was sick of finding the toilet covered in shit every morning, and he told Uncle

You're not a dog, right, and Uncle didn't answer, he was standing in ballerina position in the yard, and he looked at my brother very attentively but he didn't say anything, and my brother started to cry, and he yelled at him, and he told Uncle he was going to die if he kept up like this, but Uncle still didn't react, and it started to rain outside and my brother went out into the yard and headed straight for the cadaverous apple tree, and he clasped the trunk of the apple tree, and the tree was so stunted that he could get his hands all the way around it, and my brother started shaking the tree, and he shook it violently in his sadness and anger, and he pulled on it as hard as he could, and he twisted the trunk, and I went to my brother and I told him to stop it, to leave the trees alone, but my brother said Don't come one step closer, and his eyes were full of rage, and the rain was falling on us, and my brother pulled so hard that he fell on his bottom, then he rolled over on all fours and dug up handfuls of dirt, all the way down to the roots, and there was mud all over his pants, and he got up to pull on the tree again until he could yank it out of the ground and Uncle and I understood that my brother was trying to demolish his trees, and Uncle usually loves it when there are fights on TV and arguments at home, but watching his nephew uproot the trees he'd so carefully planted, Uncle seemed deeply troubled, and he didn't say anything, he stood in the yard next to me, and I felt a lump deep in my throat, and my brother went to the cherry tree and at first he did the same as with the apple tree, shaking the trunk, but then he pulled out the stake and pummeled the trunk with the stake, and he yelled and the stake broke in two, then my brother tore off the branches and Uncle and I watched, and it was so sad to see my brother so angry, as if everyone was his enemy, and nothing could stop him, and then I could only hope that my brother would end up wearing himself out, because I didn't dare go to him or take him in my arms, since that day he had enough rage in him to rip out all the fruit trees, and that evening my brother wasn't hungry and he wouldn't get up from the couch, and Uncle timidly asked if it was possible to order a new antenna, because things just weren't the same with no TV, and he also wanted to know if my brother and I were planning to leave once the trains started running again, and that was the first time Uncle had given any sign that he wanted us gone, and as a joke I said You want us to go, and Uncle said No no, just wondering, and we all laughed, even my brother, but deep down we were a little hurt all the same.

The fruit trees were lying on the grass in the yard like some species that grows horizontally, and every now and then my brother furtively glanced outside, Never again, he said, would he set foot in that yard he'd turned into a cemetery.

A few days later my brother made up his mind to leave, he needed a change and he wanted to see his little ladyfriend whatever it took, so he'd rented a car that he planned to drive to the Spanish border, and he said that after all those Spanish lessons he should be able to talk his way past the customs agents at the border, and he also let it be known that he couldn't take Uncle anymore—it was too hard—and we shouldn't delude ourselves, we weren't going to set him right again, and he'd been living like this for too long, like a dog or a cat or maybe a pig, and I told him that was probably true, and Uncle came downstairs to say goodbye to his nephew, and my brother put his arms around Uncle, and he patted his shoulder, telling him to take good care of himself, and Uncle said No problem, and he said he'd just seen a battle scene in a movie, blood and guts all over the place, he said excitedly, and my brother turned to me and we hugged, and I felt his tense, stiff body, as if he were stuck in the ground up to his knees, and he was just as stiff as he closed the door behind him, and even if I knew he probably hadn't yet gotten into the car I felt like he was already thousands of miles away, that he might be wanting to be alone in his agitation, and so, without really realizing it, I'd decided to stay with Uncle.

Uncle went into a pre-spring hibernation phase right after my brother left, and I could only tell he was around by the creaking floorboards, and

Uncle didn't come down to mow the lawn or shoot his bow, and he lost all interest in the mole traps whose batteries had run down, and I must say that suited me just fine.

One day, after I hadn't seen hide or scalp of Uncle for forty-eight hours, I went to the bottom of the stairs to call him, and it was starting to worry me that he didn't even come downstairs to go to the bathroom or replenish his supply of chocolate cookies, and Uncle didn't answer, and I paced around, and I told myself that after all he had the right to hide away in his room and not answer me, he didn't owe me anything, I was only his niece and he was my uncle, and then suddenly an image came back to me, an image from a recent, restless night, the image of Uncle disappearing through the plumbing, and I ran to the toilet.

I looked into the bathroom but there was nothing particularly interesting to see apart from the dull yellow wall and its fly specks and a few cobwebs in the corners, a room saturated with stagnant, slightly distant smells, ghostly smells like the traces of millions of trips to the toilet of which there remained a stench that wasn't profoundly unpleasant, just a little oppressive, impregnating the substance of the walls, and I bent over the toilet bowl, making a megaphone of my hands, and yelled Lunchtime, knowing that food attracts Uncle, and since he still didn't answer I went up to his room, and I opened the door and I saw that his room was empty, it seemed even emptier than after we cleaned it, no toys lying around, no cigarette smell, no trash on the ground, no sign of his yellow crutches, only the bow and the quiver in one corner, sitting there as if they were waiting for something, or maybe someone, and without thinking what I was doing I picked up the bow and the quiver.

And I circled the yard again and again, and I looked under the arborvitae a hundred times just to be sure, knowing that Uncle is no longer that right size to slip under the hedge like pheasants do to lay their eggs, and apart from the stones that might have been pheasant eggs just about to hatch there was nothing to see under the branches, and I started back to the house, and that was when I discovered two lines of staggered holes running from the front door to the gate, and I recognized the marks that crutches make in gravel, and I trusted in my foreboding, and I followed his footsteps.

11

I start out from the house, and the crutch prints are already getting fainter when I reach the pasture, where a bunch of horses are grazing and rubbing their noses on the fenceposts to get rid of the flies, so there's no point in asking if they happened to see a short, fat man on crutches go by, how could they, they're busy living their old-nag lives, and next to a mare there's a girl in riding clothes readying her brushes and hoof-picks, and the girl sneezes because of the pollen and the dung of the horse whose hooves she's about to clean, and I go to her and we say Hello and I ask if she might by chance have seen Uncle, a short fat man with a limp and two crutches for walking sticks, and the girl looks at me, her eyes are full of eyedrops, she tells me, which blurs her vision and no, no Uncle on crutches, maybe an aunt, an aunt, yes, but no Uncle here by the stables, and I thank her and say she should put masks on them, on her poor horses, to protect them from the flies, but she already seems to have stopped listening, she lifts the horse's leg and the horse doesn't resist, and I head toward a wheat field, and the wheat has grown tall these past few days, which troubles me, because springtime, the season of hawthorns and crickets, claims many victims all around the hamlet, and with Uncle nowhere in sight I think about the farmers, their spades, their poisonous sprays and fierce machines, and I tell myself Uncle could easily have fallen asleep in a field and, slow as he is, not managed to flee a rain of toxic chemicals, and that's all I need, Uncle among the victims of dandelion season, but, still doubting that my timorous uncle would have exposed himself to such a threat, I press on by the only route open to me, which is to say the little street that winds through the hamlet, and in front of the Charrieaus' house I run into Madame Charrieau, who's cutting her roses again, and her dog Mildiou is standing next to her, and I ask if

she might perhaps have seen Uncle, who she
knows well, having for so many years seen him
ride past on his moped, and Madame Charrieau
asks what on earth I'm doing with this bow and
these arrows, and she tells me her husband,
Monsieur Charrieau, is a seasoned hunter, a
great specialist, but he's never had anything to
do with bow hunting, she explains, on the contrary, here they have dogs to flush out the game
that Monsieur Charrieau fills with his rifle bul-
lets, the game that later ages in the basement
near Madame Charrieau's clean panties, but as it
happens Monsieur Charrieau came down with
bronchitis, then otitis, then conjunctivitis, then a
cataract, now he's blind in one eye, and he's
afraid he might shoot little Mildiou if he goes
hunting, Madame Charrieau explains, telling me
that the other day she saw Uncle still wearing
his jacket that made him look like a Medieval
hunchback, and I take the opportunity to tell her
Uncle's been missing for several hours and I'm
worried, because with his bad hip and his big
heart that won't pump right he usually sticks to
little walks along the hedge, maybe ten minutes'
walk at most, And now, Madame Charrieau, he's

already been gone for six hours, and Madame Charrieau tries to reassure me, she says he can't have got far, and she'll ask her husband to keep an eye out, but it will have to be the right eye, Madame Charrieau chuckles, and I thank her and leave her to her roses, and the little street leads to a path that runs alongside the bay, and I find it hard to imagine Uncle starting down that narrow cliffside path, crab-walking with his crutches, but that's the only way he could have gone, the dangerous way, the slippery way, the one the Charrieaus avoid for fear of broken hips, so, I tell myself, it had to be something serious to get my indolent uncle to leave the cozy squalor of his room, something very serious, because if there's one thing Uncle prizes it's his daily routine, and I tell myself I'm an idiot because I should have looked to see if he'd at least made himself a snack or if he'd at least left with a bottle of Coke, because it really wouldn't be like him to rush off without letting me know, and on foot what's more, as if all at once he'd gotten fed up, as if he couldn't go on this way, consequences be damned, he must have been sick of his family treating him like a big baby, like a puppy, and he must have wanted nothing more to do with me, I'd overstepped my boundaries and meddled in things that were none of my business, and Uncle wanted to keep living on downmarket charcuterie and chocolate bars, he wanted to keep knocking back quarts of soda, not to mention that the horrible liquid we forced him to drink, water, gave him violent diarrhea, and he couldn't see the point of washing his hands, or his feet, or the rest of him, and he didn't want to wash anymore, ever again, no, he wanted to luxuriate in his wallow, and he'd rather die than go back to the house, and I force my way through the undergrowth, which doesn't seem to have been trimmed for ages, the ferns brush my chin, the nettles and brambles come up to my shoulders, and I press my lips together to keep from swallowing a wasp or, who knows, maybe a bigger winged creature that would put a quick end to my expedition, and there's cheeping in the blackberry bushes, and there's skittering, and I use Uncle's bow like a scythe and I fell the pimpernel and the tall grass, but the growth gets denser as I go on, and the twigs slap me and scratch me, and on the tips of the fern leaves I see huge ticks swollen with deer and seagull blood, ticks full of terrible diseases just waiting to sink their rostra into the first thigh that comes along, and I feel like I'm swelling up, I feel like a slow, giant animal, as if I'd outgrown the narrow path I knew as a child, and I get down on all fours and then down on my stomach to make quicker progress, and I notice that the dirt is as populated as the air, and I run over a worm, and I run over a ground beetle, and I terrify a dung beetle, I'm starting to feel like some indescribable meat, like some ultrarare beast, but I must say, you quickly get used to that dandelion-level locomotion, that caterpillar's-eye view, and so, backhanding every obstacle aside, I crawl for what seems like hours, maybe days, but very likely my sense of time has become a snail's, and I crawl and I crawl and suddenly I see the flies, green, metallic, bronze, flies that lay eggs on food, and I see before me quite a feast, if there's one subject matter I've acquired an intimate knowledge of over the past few months it's fecal matter, specifically Uncle's, and when I see the stinking fly-infested little mound, I can say with certainty that Uncle has come this way, that he's headed for the bay, and I push on toward the rocky steps covered with lichen and seaweed, and I go down the stairs and end up in the wet sand of the bay, in the enormous, empty, refreshing void of the bay, where there's not much to see on the bed of the absent sea, two or three little rocks in the middle, and sulfur-smelling algae, and crab shells and mussel shells, and I look into the distance in search of anything moving out there, something that might be Uncle, but it's always the same, the more you look into the distance the more the horizon blurs into the sea, making what looks like a single gray wall, and inside that mirage the sounds intensify, the wind and the cries of the seagulls, and those cries, which are always very loud at first, soon get lost somewhere in the clouds, between two salty breezes, who knows, and when the gulls cry like that I tell myself there's no point going on searching, Uncle must have long since been devoured by an animal or the sea, and I'm already seeing myself turn around, tossing Uncle's bow into a bush somewhere, finding the house empty when I get back, never really able to explain what happened when someone later asks me where Uncle went, but the closer I come to the seagulls the more they cry as if there were something to eat here, and there are those rocks in the middle of the waterless bay, and under the gulls, on one of the rocks, I see two yellow crutches, and I come closer and that's when I see Uncle sitting on the rock, his crutches lying in the sand by a pile of empty whelks and a half-full bottle of Coke, and his arms are scratched up, and I scarcely dare approach Uncle, who's surrounded by a squadron of shrieking gulls, and Uncle seems to be busy with something, and when I squint as if I were contemplating a menhir in the mist I see Uncle has a little gull in his hands, and he's talking to it and caressing it, and only then do I tell myself he's alive, and with an abrupt, decisive gesture Uncle wrings the gull's neck, it cracks immediately, and the bird doesn't have a chance to defend itself, and it immediately succumbs in Uncle's palm, and as if that were the end of the show the other gulls fly off, and Uncle passes the little body from one hand to the other, as if now he could gauge its weight, and then Uncle starts taking off the yellow, which is to say the beak and the legs, which he throws onto the pile of shells, and in a flash Uncle plucks the bird, and Uncle brings it up to this face and bites into the pink, obscene flesh, and the blood flows onto Uncle's face and Uncle's hands, and I run, and I throw myself at Uncle and when he sees me coming Uncle freezes and he flinches and he even tries to hide the gull behind his back, but I saw it all and I yell at him as loud as I can, and I also remind him that the doctor forbade him to eat meat, and I look at his face smeared with blood and drool and a sort of seagull hair stuck to his lip, and caught in the act Uncle apologizes, he says he thought the doctor had only forbidden red meat, and gull isn't red meat, and he apologizes again and again, and he asks me what I was planning to do with his bow and arrow in the bay, and I don't say a word, and I look at him, and Uncle lays the seagull on the pile of shells, and the pile settles a little, and Uncle bends over and picks up the bottle of Coke, and he takes a big swig of Coke to wash down the seagull, and he drinks so fast that he burps, but not in a crude or noisy way, no, more of a discreet burp, a burp entirely inside of him, a heave.

12

Sometimes, without my having to call him, without my even hearing him come downstairs, I find Uncle sitting at the table, as if he'd found some way to fly, and often after his nap the ends of his eyebrows are turned up like horns, which means he's just woken, and when his eyebrows are turned up like that we don't talk, the only sound is our stomachs gurgling, because I know Uncle has just woken up from his nap and doesn't like to talk when he wakes up from his nap, and we rumble and whistle, and Uncle looks at the dark television screen, and after lunch Uncle stands up to go get some cheese, cutting off a fat quarter of cheese, and when the cheese is gone Uncle seems a little more awake, and he goes out into the yard.

He walks across the yard, past the ravaged fruit trees and the antenna, heads for the hedge, and when he reaches the hedge he first gets down on all fours, then lies flat on his stomach, and he crushes his stomach between him and the grass, then he stretches out his arms, and with his arms outstretched Uncle wriggles under the hedge and peers under the branches, he thrusts his hands into the brambles, and when I go to Uncle and ask what he's doing he says he's looking for eggs in the pheasants' woods, and he says their eggs look like stones, and I tell myself he might not have had enough to eat, and I squat down next to Uncle, I lie down beside him, all my weight on my hipbones, and I reach out and try to propel myself as far under the hedge as I can, and on the other side of the hedge is the road.

I hear Monsieur and Madame Charrieau talking as they walk their dog Mildiou down the road on the other side of the hedge, and Mildiou comes to a stop when he draws alongside us, and he growls and he wags his tail between the Charrieaus' ankles, and Madame Charrieau says Here Mildiou, but Mildiou doesn't listen, and he dives under the hedge and he licks Uncle's hands and he sniffs us, and he rubs against our heads and Monsieur and Madame Charrieau shout Heel Mildiou, there's nobody here anymore, you can see for yourself, only bugs and bug eggs, and the Charrieaus' voices echo and disappear in the damp air, fade into dizzying ultrasounds, distant whistles, and Mildiou, it must be said, is a deaf old dog, and he's missing one or two canine teeth, you can see it when he smiles.

Translator's notes

page 24: The ORTF ran the national French radio stations and television channels in the sixties and seventies.

page 32: A PMU (pari-mutuel urbain) is a bar that doubles as a venue for off-track betting, lottery games, and so on. PMUs are generally not noted for their charm.

page 34: Les Ramoneurs de Menhirs are a Celtic folk-punk group, particularly popular in Brittany, many of whose songs are sung in the Breton language. A menhir is a standing stone of the sort widely found in Brittany; a *ramoneur* is a chimney sweep. It is of course not possible to sweep the interior of a menhir.

page 34: EDF is the French national electric company; Jardiland and M. Bricolage are big-box stores (gardening and hardware, respectively); Moto Évasion would be a motorcycle shop, in this case in the Breton town of Plancoët.

page 118: "Mildew" is both the English meaning and the pronunciation of the French "Mildiou," but a French reader would also see in that name a play on Milou, the name of intrepid white dog in the *Tintin* comic-book series.

Rebecca Gisler, born in Zurich in 1991, is a graduate of the Swiss Literature Institute and of the Master's degree in Création littéraire at the University of Paris 8. She writes in German and French and translates her texts from one language into another. She has published poetry and prose in numerous magazines and anthologies. She is the co-organizer of the series Teppich in the House of Literature Zürich. In 2020, Rebecca Gisler won the 28th Open Mike literature competition.

Jordan Stump is a professor of French at the University of Nebraska-Lincoln, the author of two book-length studies of the writing of Raymond Queneau (*Naming and Unnaming* and *The Other Book*), and the translator of some thirty works of mostly contemporary French fiction, by such authors as Marie NDiaye, Scholastique Mukasonga, Eric Chevillard, and Marie Redonnet. His translation of Marie NDiaye's *The Cheffe* won the American Literary Translators' Association prize for prose in 2020.